AI

Brandon Fisher FBI Series
Eleven
Silent Graves
The Defenseless
Blue Baby
Violated
Remnants
On the Count of Three

Detective Madison Knight Series
Ties That Bind
Justified
Sacrifice
Found Innocent
Just Cause
Deadly Impulse
In the Line of Duty
Power Struggle
Shades of Justice
Life Sentence

McKinley Mysteries
The Day Job is Murder
Vacation is Murder
Money is Murder
Politics is Murder
Family is Murder
Shopping is Murder
Christmas is Murder
Valentine's Day is Murder
Skiing is Murder
Halloween is Murder
Exercise is Murder

Matthew Connor Adventure Series
City of Gold
The Secret of the Lost Pharaoh

Assassination of a Dignitary

Coffee is Murder

INTERNATIONAL BESTSELLING AUTHOR
Carolyn Arnold

HIBBERT & STILES
PUBLISHING INC.

Hibbert & Stiles Publishing Inc.
www.hspubinc.com

Names: Arnold, Carolyn.
Title: Coffee is Murder / Carolyn Arnold.
Description: [London, Ontario] : Hibbert & Stiles Publishing Inc., [2015] | Series: McKinley Mystery series [book 9]
Identifiers: ISBN 9781988064925 (4 x 6 paperback) | ISBN 9781989706107 (5 x 8 paperback) | ISBN 9781507017814 (ebook)

Coffee is Murder

Chapter 1

A Moment of Appreciation

For Sara, coffee was one of life's greatest—and simplest—pleasures. Every time she took a draw of freshly brewed java, her eyelids automatically lowered in appreciation of the robust flavor. Somehow, when drinking it, life seemed less complicated, or maybe it was just how it coated the palate and calmed her nerves despite what some scientific studies might say.

She was in her home office, seated behind her desk, staring at the blinking cursor on her monitor, but it wasn't because she had writer's block. Her wrists needed a break. Better yet, she needed to indulge in this cup.

Leaning back in her chair, she swiveled from side to side and closed her eyes, savoring the aroma of the dark beans. While they were ground at the time she pressed the button, the only way to get it any fresher was picking the beans off the plants in Brazil. With their money, she supposed it was an option.

She let herself get caught up with the thought. It might not be a bad idea. As her daydreaming grew in scale, she laughed. She wasn't going to board a plane to South America for a cup of coffee, even though it might be the best she'd ever had. She wasn't that obsessed—was she?

Sean knocked, but entered without awaiting a reply. He held on to a glass of orange juice and she admired his self-restraint. For some reason, his body required only one coffee a day when he first woke up. Otherwise, he moved on to juice or water.

If Sean had his way, Sara would drink only one, but coffee was a habit she wasn't willing to break. Maybe she was an addict, although, that word carried such a negative connotation. She wasn't an alcoholic simply because she enjoyed an evening beverage, so her coffee indulgence shouldn't be considered an addiction. Even her thoughts betrayed her. *Indulgence.*

"Good morning, darling." Sean kissed her forehead and then her lips. "I hope I'm not interrupting." He glanced at the screen. "I guess I'm not."

She smirked at him, realizing only a chapter number was showing. "I'm just taking a small break. I can't always be typing, you know. I'm not a machine."

"The way you've been holed up in here lately, I'm starting to wonder."

She pouted. "Are you feeling lonely?"

"A little bit like a writer's widower actually."

"Well, let me make it up to you." She stood, cupped his face with her hands, and kissed his mouth.

When they parted, any pleasure she derived from the coffee had diluted. It was replaced by the need to hold her husband.

"Hmm. Not bad," he said.

"Excuse me?"

"You have coffee breath. I have orange juice breath. Still, the kiss, not bad."

She narrowed her eyes and was about to say something when the phone on her desk rang.

Sean answered. "Hello…yes, Helen…all right, make the appointment for two hours from now."

As she listened to her husband speak, she had a good idea what this was about. There was a job.

Chapter 2

The Organization

Sean and Sara had their private investigator licenses and had decided to open a firm. They didn't want to work from home, even though it was quite likely there would be some crossover. The building was more or less a meeting place for clients. While she, Sean, Jimmy, and Adam had offices there, they would only go in when there was a case.

Jimmy had a barebones office, designed to his liking, which afforded him a wooden desk, a desktop computer, two vertical filing cabinets, and a colored print on the wall. The latter was non-negotiable. Just because the man had simpler taste didn't mean the place couldn't be classy.

Contrasting to Jimmy's office, Adam's space had state-of-the-art everything. Adam, who they had brought on board from their New York company, Universal Acquisitions, spent most of his time in the Big Apple. They had given him a promotion and he was in charge of Internet security—a task he was more than qualified for. He was a genius, another reason they needed him on their team. When required, he came out to Albany.

Sara and Sean shared a sizable office with two work stations, each with a desktop computer.

The front reception desk was where Helen spent Mondays through Fridays, from ten until three. She had a young daughter, Mia, who, at only six years old, had fought cancer and won. The limited hours allowed Helen time to pick Mia up from kindergarten and get over to the McKinleys' to tidy their house and prepare dinner. As things grew with the agency, Sara wouldn't be surprised if Helen requested to work there full-time. And the search for a maid would be on once again.

At the agency, Helen's responsibilities included answering the phones, filtering through case applications, paperwork, and bookkeeping. If Helen was calling now—and Sean had agreed to a meeting in a couple hours—Helen had deemed a case a priority.

There were two criteria they provided her to determine urgency. One, the police had closed their investigation, yet circumstances surrounding the death were suspicious. And two, the applicant needed to note three charities to receive a portion of the business's earnings. If people couldn't bring themselves to list three notable causes, then why should they invest their time to help them?

Sean hung up. "We might have our first official case."

"I gathered that."

"I'd say your gift of intuition was remarkable, but in this situation—"

"Yes, it was rather easy. So, what is it?"

"In brief, a woman lost her mother two weeks ago. The police fail to acknowledge foul play because no one stood out as wanting to hurt the woman."

"So no autopsy?"

"Not on the city's dime anyway. The daughter paid for one, but nothing was found."

"Why does she believe her mother was murdered?"

"Because she was complaining of dizziness and nausea the week before her death. It was thought she had the flu."

"I hate to say it, Sean, but the flu can kill people."

"It can, but the flu doesn't typically cause stomach or intestinal problems in adults."

"Really? I thought that vomiting was one of the main symptoms."

"I guess it's not. The daughter is a nurse and says she knows this."

"Then why not take her mother to a doctor to get whatever she had diagnosed?"

"She was going to, but her mother died before the appointment."

Chapter 3

Living the Dream

Their firm was located on Broadway, which was part of the downtown historic district. It was just a small postage-stamp-sized property nestled between the Broadway Plaza and another building. Despite the fact that they could have afforded a larger space—the entire block if they were so inclined—the size of their building was more than sufficient.

Sara found the curb appeal to be quaint and cozy, almost the feel of an old book store. The architecture was unique, with arched window frames and a decorative cap at the top of the structure that complimented the style of the façade. They used the main level and basement for their offices. In total, the building was four stories tall. The layout was suited to leasing out the other levels, as there was a separate entrance around back. They preferred to work with one or more non-profit organizations just starting out. They would offer the space at an affordable monthly amount.

It wasn't as if she and Sean needed the money, but their accountant had insisted that the business carry its own weight. They had chosen not to draw a salary, but the cost of labor and materials needed to be billed out, just as any private investigator agency. Where their financial management clashed was that after expenses were covered, the remainder was divvied up to the charities specified on their customer's application.

While the client wrote one check, their accountant ensured that the amounts were distributed accordingly.

The doorbell chimed when they entered.

The front entrance was a wall of windows with green trim, and the lettering on them announced their hours along with their phone number. The firm's name was still being decided, and Sara was ashamed by her lack of creativity when it came to picking one. She had a feeling they'd end up settling on something basic and relatively generic like McKinley Private Investigators. Right now it read *Private Investigators.*

Helen was on the phone, but acknowledged them with a bob of her head. "Yes, I can send you an application. Complete that and send it back to us, and I assure you it will receive top priority when it comes in. How would you like to receive the application? Email, fax, mail, or you can pick one up in person….sure, I will send it shortly."

Sara smiled at Sean. All of this felt right. Just like slipping into an old pair of favorite jeans or spending a Sunday morning lounging around in pajamas. Opening this firm was the right decision. They had a talent for solving murders. Why waste that skill when so many needed closure and justice for a loved one?

"You can just attach it and reply to the email I send you or deliver it in person, whatever you wish. All right, yes…okay…" As Helen carried on the conversation with the caller, Sara analyzed the space.

The interior designers had certainly accomplished the task assigned them. Sara was adamant that the agency not resemble the PI offices on TV or in the movies, which were all dark, drab, and depressing. And, as if the dark colors weren't enough, they were finished off with bulky pieces of furniture and cluttered desks.

Here, it was the stark opposite. Bright lighting bathed the space, and it was furnished with sleek lines of white and chrome. The walls were neutral with dabs of color coming from accent pieces and framed, abstract paintings with large swaths of reds, blues, and yellows. This theme followed through the space on both levels.

Behind reception a feature wall was turquoise, a color known for its soothing and calm energy. People who came here had gone through a lot and it would be comforting to them.

"Sounds good, Ms. Carter, I will watch for it. Thank you…Good day." Helen returned the receiver and crossed her eyes. "It's been a busy morning."

Sara drew her gaze from their framed licenses, which stood out against the blue-green wall. "I'm not sure if that's a good thing or not." Her response was spoken without thought, but one of the factors that had initially held them back from opening a business was the potential workload. It didn't seem to matter if they were officially in business or not, murder tended to find them. It was best to keep busy in life anyway, especially when one was given a gift. She noticed both Sean and Helen were watching her. "Although, the more cases we have applications for, the more will be approved, and the more charities will benefit."

"I think it's beautiful what you're doing with the profits."

"It's just the right thing to do."

"Still, it's nice."

Sean put his hand on Sara's lower back. "When will our client be in?"

"You said two hours, Mr. McKinley, and that's exactly when I booked her for. You still have an hour to review the file." She handed Sean a manila folder. "This is her application. It also contains my notes, of course."

When Helen deemed a case worthy of their attention, she'd conduct preliminary work which included pulling financial information on the applicant, the deceased's past as well as their obituary, and the official ruling on cause of death.

"Thank you, Helen. You're doing a great job," Sara said.

"Thank you." Helen's cheeks blushed.

Sara recognized her reaction for what it was. Helen was industrious and thorough, but had a hard time taking compliments. Work was something Helen just did without contestation or the need for praise. She was the type that made things appear easy to everyone else. It was a quality often taken advantage of in the professional arena. Here, she would never have that problem.

Chapter 4

Blond and Determined

Sean and Sara took the file to the meeting room, which had a glass table and seating for six. The space had more sleek lines and chrome. A large screen was on one wall—the modern-day solution to a marker board. Adam's enthusiasm about the technology of the interactive whiteboard was contagious and had Sean parting with the money.

Every time Sean entered the room, though, he was glad that he had made the investment. Adam's praise was well-deserving. The board served a decorative purpose and was practical. Unlike the traditional predecessor, with this electronic one, it was possible to save any notes or doodles as images and PDFs.

Sean handed Sara the file. She was a faster reader, so, once she finished reading a sheet, she would pass it on to him and keep going. They still had more to read when two shadows graced the doorway.

It was Helen and a pretty blonde, who, Sean assumed, must be their prospective client, Sophie Hogan. He had read enough of the preliminary. Between the application and what Helen had told him, he was aware Sophie worked as a nurse in a retirement home. It was her mother, Beverly Sparks, who'd passed away. She was sixty-nine at the time of her death.

"Sean, Sara, this is Sophie Hogan." Helen conducted the formal introductions as she guided the woman farther into the room.

"Hello. Nice to meet you both. Thank you for agreeing to take my case." Sophie shook Sean's hand.

He didn't have the heart to correct her assumption. This meeting was a preliminary interview. She had made it past Helen, and now he and Sara had to decide if they'd accept the case, or if there even was one to take on.

Sophie clasped Sara's hand in greeting now. "You are beautiful."

"Thank you. So are you."

Sean never tired of people saying that to his wife. She was attractive both inside and outside and had a quality that drew people. Jealousy periodically slipped in when it involved men, but he was working to root out the undesirable quality.

Sophie's head dipped and she pulled out a chair, but hesitated. "I guess I shouldn't assume. Is it all right if I sit here?"

"Of course." Sara spoke gently and Sean admired, again, his wife's ability to put people at ease.

Sophie was positioned across from them so it worked out ideally. Eye contact and being able to read a person's body language was a big factor in conversation. Often, more was said through energy and movement than was communicated through words.

"I'm going to excuse myself, if that will be all." Helen waved a hand, pointing toward the door.

"That will be. Thank you, Helen," Sean said.

She closed the door behind her, and Sean settled his gaze on Sophie. She was thirty-two, according to the file, but she could have passed for mid-twenties. Her eyes were hazel and her hair was bottle-blond with dark lowlights. She wore it down at the back with the sides pulled up and clipped into a barrette. As a generalization, women freed their face of wandering strands when they were focused. And, despite her timorous mannerisms, Sean saw a person who was likely confident in her own right. He figured that consulting with private investigators ventured outside of most people's comfort zones.

The business had opened its doors a month ago and had come together rather quickly—money equaled power, and, when the contractors found out it was multi-billionaire Sean McKinley requesting their services, they were more than efficient. A job that might have stretched out for months if they were working for someone else was condensed to the timespan of thirty days.

Three months ago, they had bought the property. Two months ago, they had hired the contractor. And one month ago, they had officially opened the doors. With the applications coming in from the moment they'd purchased the property, they were ready to start as soon as they found a case that matched their criteria.

"Would you like a cup of coffee or a glass of water?" Sara asked her.

Sophie shook her head. "Your assistant did ask me, but I'm good. I'm off coffee right now."

"All right, well, we've read a good portion of your file and application, but it's much better to hear things straight from the person. First of all, you have our sympathies for your loss," Sean said.

Sophie's lips quivered and she nodded.

"You don't believe it was related to her age."

She slid her bottom lip through her teeth. "Not at all. My mother was in good physical shape. She might not have been very active, but she was sixty-nine. Still, considering her age and all she had gone through in life, she had many more years left." Her voice fractured on the last sentence.

"You're saying that she was murdered?" Sara's tone was soft.

"That's exactly what I'm saying."

Chapter 5

Special Memories

Sophie's response didn't come as a surprise. After all, people didn't seek them out when they felt their loved ones had passed away peacefully. They sought them out to get answers they weren't getting elsewhere.

Sara crossed her legs underneath the table and leaned forward. She considered taking another sip of her coffee, but decided against it. "Tell us about your mother."

"You mean, did she have anyone who didn't like her?"

Sara nodded. This woman was sharp. Despite Sara's initial assessment that her loss had shaken her spirit, the truth couldn't be further from that evaluation.

"No, not that I knew. My mother was a kind woman, soft spoken, thoughtful. Half the time she'd be out in the neighborhood picking up people's recycling boxes for them. She didn't need to do that, but she said she wanted to do her part."

"She picked up their recycling boxes?" Sean queried further.

"You know how you set it out on the curb and—well, maybe you don't."

Sara felt her cheeks heat. "We do know." She glanced at Sean, who appeared to be equally embarrassed by being categorized into the rich and naïve segment of society.

"We weren't always—" Sara rolled her hand, hoping that Sophie would pick up and save her from putting things bluntly.

"That's right. You're weren't always rich. I apologize."

Sara was wearing a blazer with a long-sleeve blouse, and this conversation was making her warm and uncomfortable. People who had limited means complained that judgment was unduly passed on them. Until now, Sara never realized how the reverse was also true. It didn't matter who you were or what you had, people always had an opinion to offer. Typically it was fired from the other end of the spectrum based on nothing more than fabricated conjecture. It was a sad reality of mankind.

Sophie continued. "On recycling day, after the boxes and garbage receptacles were emptied, my mother took them from the curb and put them in front of her neighbors' doors."

"What a sweet woman." Sara's automatic reaction had Sean smiling at her.

"Yes, she was, and I can't imagine anyone wanting to hurt her, let alone kill her."

The file held the answer to her next question, but Sara wanted to hear it from Sophie. "Your mother was found in her home?"

"That's right. She…" Sophie's voice hitched and was gravelly, but she continued, "was found in her favorite chair by the window. She always loved watching the world go by. She was a real people watcher."

Sean shuffled some paperwork on the table and lifted a sheet. "The autopsy shows cause of death as respiratory failure."

"That's what it says."

"You don't believe that part to be true?"

Sophie looked between them. “I’m not sure about that part, but if she did just stop breathing, it wasn’t because it was her time.” She pulled out a tissue from her purse and dabbed the corners of her eyes. “It wasn’t the flu either. I was going to take her to the doctor and have him tell her. I didn’t want to be the one to say what I thought it really was.”

“And what’s that?” Sara asked.

“I’m a nurse. You probably saw that in the file. Well, normal flu symptoms in an adult include fever, headache, fatigue, cough, sore throat, runny or stuffy nose, and body aches. Vomiting isn’t a symptom, despite popular belief. It is more likely in children, but my mother also had dizziness and winded easily.” She paused, and when she seemed certain she had their full attention, she said, “My mother was poisoned with cyanide.”

With Sophie laying out her diagnosis so pointedly, Sara swallowed deeply. She couldn’t imagine stating the cause of her mother’s death so calmly. Maybe it had to do with Sophie’s medical background.

“Cyanide? Why do you figure that specifically?” Sean asked.

“The symptoms line up.”

“But you said that no one would dislike your mother enough to kill her.”

“Oh, I never said that she was targeted, but I do believe she was murdered.”

Sara was certain her facial expression reflected her confusion.

Sophie elaborated. “I don’t think she was necessarily targeted, per se, but the poisoning resulted in her death nonetheless. The doctor was always saying that all that coffee would kill her someday.”

"Her coffee?" Sara pushed her mug down the table. The thought of dying as a result of drinking it took away any desire to finish it off.

"Yeah, she drank five, six, cups a day. She found joy in it. That, reading, and watching her soaps."

Sara ignored the sideways glance Sean shot her.

"You think someone poisoned her coffee?"

"I do, but I don't think it was someone she knew. I think it came to her poisoned."

Chapter 6

A Baggie of Beans

Sean filled a glass with water from the cooler and placed it in front of Sara. "Came to her poisoned?"

"Yes, and this is where I feel remorse." Sophie stopped talking as she sobbed for a few seconds.

Sean hoped that after all of this, Sara might view the habit differently and opt for a lower caffeine beverage like tea, or skip the caffeine altogether.

Sophie patted her nose with the tissue and then cleared her throat. "I got her a gift for Christ—" A hiccup. "I'm so—" Another hiccup. She held up her finger and her cheeks blew out.

This wasn't the time to find humor, but Sean couldn't help it. Sophie was a pretty woman, but with her cheeks flared out like a chipmunk with its mouth full of nuts, well…

She let out a rush of air. "Okay, I think they're gone. I got my mother a coffee of the month membership."

Sara leaned farther across the table, and Sean put his hand on her shoulder to draw her back. She followed his prompting, but not without narrowing her eyes at him.

"There's a coffee club?" Despite the fact Sara had settled against the back of her chair, her tone held wonder and fascination.

Maybe Sara wasn't rethinking her coffee habit after all.

"I've never heard of such a thing. It sounds like the perfect gift for the coffee lover."

He turned away when Sara tried to meet his eyes.

Sophie didn't seem to pick up on any of their nonverbal communication and continued. "The company is Tasty Beans. They specialize in flavored coffee. For a fee, they will even make one to order."

"You mentioned a coffee of the month," Sean prompted her to expound.

"Members are allowed a pound per month, in whatever flavor they wish. My mother activated her membership on January first, and the only reason she waited that long was because they had shut down for the holidays. But ever since she activated, she ordered their specialty flavor, which was dark cherry almond."

Sean expected a moan, or some sort of reaction from his java-addicted wife, but instead, she crossed her arms.

"You think the beans were poisoned?" she asked.

"I do. Now, I don't know if they were shipped that way from the company, or something happened along the way."

Sean interjected. "But you don't think someone did it on this end?"

Sophie shook her head.

"So that leaves either the coffee company or the shipping company."

"That's what I think."

"Have you had the coffee tested?"

Sophie pulled her purse from the floor and produced a baggie of beans. "I have no idea where to get something like that done. I was hoping you could help with that."

"I'm sure we could."

"So, that's pretty much all I know. Are you able to

help me find out exactly what happened to my mother? The police don't want to hear from me anymore. Every time I follow up with Detective Griffith, he sighs deeply into the phone. It's heartbreaking and exasperating."

Griffith was a tool when Sean worked with him. He was the type of person that only saw the negative in life and refused to allow room for the positive. "I'm sure it's not personal. Everyone has things going on in their life." He was quick to add, "Not that it's professional behavior by any means."

"Are you going to take my case?" Sophie's eyes brimmed with tears, making it nearly impossible to say no.

"Why do you believe someone poisoned the coffee?" Sara asked.

"It's a feeling, but my mother's diet didn't change. She was always eating organic and whole foods. The only thing that was different was the coffee."

Until they had the coffee tested, poisoning couldn't be confirmed. If the results were negative, there wasn't much of anything to investigate. Although Sophie seemed adamant that her mother was murdered, Sean was about to answer from the standpoint of logic—they'd get the beans tested and go from there, but Sara responded first.

"We'd love to help you. You just hang in there, all right?"

"Thank you. If you need anything, night or day, call me. I am back to work, so you might have to leave a message, but I will return your call as soon as I can." Sophie stood and clutched the strap of her purse, which now hung over her shoulder. "Do I give the deposit check to Helen?"

"That works."

Chapter 7

Discussing the Forensics

After Sophie had left, Sara dumped her coffee down the kitchenette's sink. Sean had followed her. It was just a basic break room—a sink, a fridge, a small counter, and a round table with seating for four. There was a toaster, a microwave, and a coffee maker on the counter.

"We don't even know if there is a case, darling." He came up behind her and wrapped his arms around her waist.

She spun to face him, staying in his embrace. "I trust her when she says her mother was murdered."

"Maybe she knows for certain because—"

"Because she did it? Is that what you were going to say?" Sara laughed.

"We need to get those beans tested and go from there. We should have waited until the results came back on that before we gave her false hope."

Sara put her hand on Sean's cheek and peered into his eyes. His logic periodically blinded him to the benefits of emotion. While some might argue whether or not it was given to humans for a reason, it served as a sort of inborn guidance system. "You did see the pictures of her mother?"

The question seemed to catch him off guard. "Her picture?"

"Yes." Sara slipped from Sean's arms and took a seat

at the table.

He sat across from her, not seeming to follow her line of thought.

"Beverly Sparks may have been sixty-nine, but there wasn't a touch of gray in her hair. She was a redhead."

"She dyed it?"

"Nope. According to the detailed autopsy report she didn't."

"Wow. I hope I still have a full head of brown hair when I'm that age."

She angled her head to peek at his sideburns. "I think it might be a little late to make that wish, sweetheart."

"Hmm." He glanced away briefly. "It still doesn't mean that her death wasn't the result of natural causes. Young people die of heart attacks these days."

"She didn't die of a heart attack though. She simply stopped breathing. It's just Sophie's conviction. She feels it in her soul that her mother was killed. She came to us for help, and I think we can offer that."

His eyes softened but the tender glaze was gone when he spoke. "I noticed that Albert Needham conducted the autopsy. It's someone we know anyway, but wouldn't he be able to detect cyanide if it had been present? I never worked a case like this before. Did you?"

She nodded. It was from before she came to Albany, but her memory was nearly flawless, so she remembered the case clearly. The victim was a mother of three children—all under the age of six. She was on subsidy and barely scraping by. While, at first, the cause of death pointed to murder by her ex, it turned out she had poisoned herself. An exact year and a day before she died, she had taken out an insurance policy that covered suicide. She must have felt like a failure to her children and figured they'd be better off without her.

Such a sad, tragic situation.

"Sara?"

"Yes. I have come across this before."

"And?"

She recollected the autopsy, being in the room, watching it play out, but primarily she remembered the smell. "It is possible that, during autopsy, there is a bitter-almond odor, but this isn't always detected. Other ways of telling are the color of the blood and the skin color. But if she was poisoned over a period of time, it might not show in either."

"Then we are back to the daughter's feeling."

"And don't forget the beans." Sara held up the baggie.

"Speaking of coffee—"

"Don't you even say it, Sean. These are flavored beans. I would never touch flavored. Why ruin coffee like that?"

Chapter 8

An Unfavorable Request

Jimmy woke up and a huge yawn ate his face. Even though he was living a dream, he found it hard to pull himself out of bed some mornings. He blamed it on his age.

It was a good thing that Meredith didn't seem to notice that he wasn't at his peak—and if she had, she didn't give any impression that it bothered her. They had been dating for over five months now, and he couldn't believe how fast the time was passing. But they had decided to take things slow. Both had been hurt before and both had gone through a divorce. Jimmy had assumed the role of victim for years, but with this spark of love back in his life, he viewed it as a blessing, an awakening of sorts. He'd always love Clara, but it was time to let her go from his heart.

His cell rang on his nightstand and he grabbed it. "Hey-lo."

"Jimmy?"

"You called his number." It was Sean and he always derived pleasure from giving the kid a hard time. The fact that he was a big kid was irrelevant. When one was young enough to be your son, you earned the right to think of them that way.

"You're pretty sharp considering you probably just woke up."

"Hey, I resemble that remark."

Sean laughed. "I thought so. Listen, we've got ourselves a case."

"I'm listening." He willed the foggy haze of just waking up to go away but it wasn't happening quickly. He put a hand to his forehead to fend off the inevitable headache that came with rushing to his feet. Life was always so kindly reminding him he wasn't in his twenties anymore, or his forties for that matter.

He listened as Sean explained about Sophie Hogan and her mother, Beverly Sparks.

"Poor girl, losing one's parent is one of the hardest things to go through in life."

The line fell silent and Jimmy could have hit himself—hard. Sean was aware of that grief all too well. His mom died when he was nine, and his father when he was twenty-two.

"I'm sorry, Sean."

"No, no, don't mention it. But, yes, I'd have to agree. Anyway, we need you to work today, if you can."

"I'd be happy to." Another stupid thing to say considering the circumstances. Maybe he should keep his mouth shut today.

"Good. We need you to talk to Albert Needham."

The name settled in the pit of his stomach. He wished he had heard wrong. Albert Needham was a medical examiner in Albany. He was crass and, from that standpoint, was in the right profession. It wasn't possible to insult the dead. Unfortunately, those who needed answers from him about the dead, well, that was a different story. They were subjected to his gruff and apathetic nature.

Sean continued. "We need you to ask him about the findings on Beverly Sparks."

"You don't have a copy of the autopsy report?" He

didn't want to be difficult, but if there was any possible way to weasel out of talking to the old coot, he was going to take advantage of it.

"We do, but we need you to speak with him. Specifically, in regards to smell."

"Smell?"

"Sophie believes her mother was poisoned with cyanide."

"You want to know if he picked up on a bitter-almond odor."

"Yes, that's right."

"I've run into it before. Remember how long I was a cop before you stole me away."

"Stole you? You didn't run?"

"Well, maybe a bit of that too." Jimmy chuckled. The sleepy haze was finally lifting.

"So, can you do that for us?"

"I'm all over it."

He ended the call, recalling the way most conversations with Sean used to conclude when Jimmy was the sergeant and Sean and Sara were his detectives. Most of the time Jimmy added *No one dies today.* It was the mantra he subscribed to and tried to pass on to those under him.

While it held a lot of purpose at the time—with his people going out and facing killers and the like—it still had merit today. Even though the three of them had left the police force, they still hunted killers and brought them to justice. That job wasn't a safe one no matter how you sliced it.

Chapter 9

A Baggie and a Plan

Jimmy's words ricocheted in Sean's head. *Losing one's parent is one of the hardest things to go through in life.* With the statement reflecting back on his own life, the essence of this case was finally making an impact. Sophie Hogan was after closure and satisfactory answers. From the law-enforcement standpoint, the truth was likely being buried beneath bureaucratic response and budgetary constraints—two things that didn't hold him or Sara back.

Sean was driving Sara, and the beans, to the laboratory. From their days as cops they had connections who could make things happen. If friendship or respect weren't enough motivation, Sean had enough money to line pockets and pay for answers. The city was always revising its budget and making cuts. The offer of compensating—generously—for results would be a welcome one.

"Are you sure Dee Dee's going to help us?" Sara asked from the passenger seat.

Dee Dee's real name was Diane Dunn, but the nickname had stuck.

"Of course she will."

"Someone's confident."

He gripped the wheel a little tighter, flexing his fingers against the leather. "I know what it's like to lose a parent. Actually, I know what it's like to lose two. I can understand why Sophie wants answers and I'm determined to find them for her."

Sara touched his forearm and her caring stroke moved him to release one hand from the wheel and reach for hers.

She didn't need to say anything and he didn't need to continue. She understood him and his past better than anyone but himself. His wife had a way of reaching into his soul and reading his spirit.

He turned the Mercedes SLS AMG GT a little too fast into the mouth of the lab's parking lot and the car angled to the left, only straightening out once the wheels had. "Are you sure you don't miss yours?"

"Are you kidding me? I could get a new one in a heartbeat. I believe there's enough in the bank." She giggled.

"There is room in the garage for more than a couple, you know."

"Sean, are you being materialistic?"

"No, I'm just saying." He smirked as he pulled into a spot and parked the car.

"I don't think it's a bad idea to get a practical one for us to do our sleuthing in."

"Don't take this one away from me."

With its gullwing doors, it didn't really fall into the practical category, but it sure was a fun ride. They had bought two, but Sara had given hers to Jimmy at Christmas. Since then, she hadn't bothered to get a vehicle of her own, but seeing as they were together most of the time, it hadn't yet proved to be an inconvenience.

He walked around to get her door. Opening it, he appreciated the view of his wife's legs—ironically, modesty was one of the reasons she preferred not to have the car—as she flung the first one out and then the second.

Her heels were three-inch stilettos, but based on the way she'd glide over the ground, she might as well have been born with them on her feet. Her skirt came past her knees but with the low ride of the car, it flashed more skin than she preferred. He, on the other hand, benefited.

She put her hand in his extended one. "I see that look on your face, mister."

"Yes, darling, but we do have a murder to solve."

She looped her arm through his. "There's my man."

He leaned his head over and rested it against hers, and they strolled like that for a couple steps. Until she stopped.

"Uh-oh."

He turned to face her. "Uh-oh?"

"Yeah, I think you're forgetting that Dee Dee was in love with you."

Come to think of it, he had thwarted Dee Dee's advances more times than possible to count and now he was going to ask a favor of her, with his bride by his side. To top off the proverbial sundae, abundant wealth was the cherry.

"Maybe I am wrong. She might not help us."

Sara put her hands on his shoulders and brushed them down the sleeves of his suit jacket. Her touch was no longer calming. Anyone in their right mind was afraid of Dee Dee—how could he have forgotten his particular reason?

"Maybe it's best I hang out here and have you handle this solo."

"Nuh-uh. We're in this together, darling, for better or for worse, remember?"

"But Big Dee?"

Sara dropped her arms. "You didn't just say that."

"I did." He winced under her gaze. Maybe that wasn't how he'd feel about Dee Dee now, but when he was single, well, she was a big woman. In retrospect, he might have been a little shallow.

"I can count on you to be respectful? Maybe I should do this alone."

"It's all right. A long time has passed. She's probably forgotten all about it."

"About what, darling?"

"Not important. Let's go." Sean grabbed her hand and led the way. He was glad when her strides kept up with his.

Chapter 10

Prepared and Armed

Not only was Jimmy going to face Needham, he was going to question his findings. The implication behind the inquiries wouldn't be lost on the medical examiner. He would see them as an accusation that he wasn't thorough at his job.

The day had started off with such promise. Jimmy had slept in and woken up when his body stirred him, and any day that happened after the sun had risen was a special day. But it had taken a quick turn as soon as he'd answered his phone. Maybe he should have let it ring to voice mail.

Now he was in his car and the clock on the dash read eleven thirty.

He'd told Sean he'd see Needham, but not immediately. He wasn't in any rush. Part of the procrastination might have been his trying to scheme his way out of this obligation. If only there was another way to twist things so he wouldn't have to face the man. He refused to disappoint Sean and Sara though. With that being the alternative he'd have to suck it up and get this done. He did give his word, and honoring that determined the worth of the man. That was something he had picked up from his pop.

"And may he rest in peace." Old habits died hard—or not at all—from Jimmy's experience, and he found himself making the sign of the cross on his chest as he mumbled the phrase.

The delicatessen was open across the street from the morgue and that would be Jimmy's first stop.

He parked the Mercedes in the city lot, against his better judgment. People were careless and held little regard for cars that weren't theirs, especially for ones like his.

Ten minutes later he was armed with the medical examiner's favorite lunch. Jimmy didn't much worry about Needham recognizing it as a bribery tactic. Basically whatever worked was fair game.

"Jimmy Voigt?" Vicki, the lady from the front desk, flashed him a smile. She was in her late forties and the two of them had always gotten along as friends. She was married to her high school sweetheart and proved that betting in favor of the odds sometimes paid off.

"In the flesh." He grinned and gestured down his outfit. Dressed in a tailored suit complete with Prada Cap-toe Balmorals, he was feeling pretty dapper. Based on her facial reaction, there was a good reason he did.

"You're looking marvelous, Jimmy. Retirement is suiting you well. I heard you left the department."

"You heard right about my no longer being with the department. The retirement part, well, that's debatable."

"Ah, so you're here on business? It wasn't to see me?"

"Sorry to disappoint, doll." He felt as if he'd been sucked back into the past. Vicki loved classic movies, like Jimmy, and they'd made small talk about them on previous occasions. Jimmy's wife had never understood what he saw in them, but for him, those films represented a time period when guys were gentlemen and dames were ladies.

"Whatcha here for?" Her eyes fell to the white paper bag he held. The name of the deli was scrawled on an angle. “You’re here to see Albert.”

“I’m afraid I am.”

“Well, I would be afraid. He’s in a rare mood, even for him. Speaking of retirement, if one person could benefit…”

“Albert?”

“No, me. So I wouldn’t have to work with him.” She chuckled at her own joke. “Do you want me to let him know you’re coming down?”

“And give him a chance to run? No way.” Jimmy tapped the counter and left for the elevator.

He wondered just how far he’d go for the McKinleys. Of course, his efforts were always acknowledged, and they had done so much for him. Needham was just an old man who was elbows deep into cadavers. Nothing to fear—right?

Chapter 11

Facing the Past

Dee Dee was standing just inside her office door and backed up to give them room to enter. She didn't offer for them to take a seat in the chairs meant for visitors. And she didn't make any move to sit herself.

"Look at who we have here." Dee Dee was in a thigh-length lab coat with something sticking out of a side pocket and pens were clipped inside the one on her chest. But Sean's observation wasn't so much on what the woman was wearing but on her size.

Dee Dee let her eyes fall over Sara and then they scrutinized Sean. "Yes, I lost weight. I'm looking fabulous, aren't I? It's not really a question. I know I am."

So much for modesty, but given her transformation Sean didn't blame her one bit. This version was easily a size six, and a hundred and twenty-five pounds. To top it off, her cheeks held a healthy glow and her skin appeared younger and hydrated. Dee Dee had worked for her new figure the old-fashioned way—healthy eating and exercise.

"You are looking fabulous. Isn't she, Sean?" Sara put her hand in his and he realized that he was standing there staring.

"She's right. You are." He fumbled with the words but got them out.

"Yeah, yeah. I bet you're having regrets now."

Sara tugged softly on Sean's arm.

"Do you realize the last time I saw this guy, I asked him out on a date? He didn't say no. He said, 'You never know, we might bump into each other at Lou's.' That's this bar downtown. So I get all dolled up and go out. I left the girlfriends at home, thinking I was going to have myself a great night out. But guess what?" She paused, ensuring she'd hooked Sara's attention. "He didn't show."

He wasn't going to be put on the spot like this. "We've been through this, Diane."

"See, he's pulling out the real name now. I make him nervous."

Sean caught the lift of Sara's lips. At least she was finding amusement over the situation.

"You don't make me nervous."

"I think you're lying. Anyway, the next thing I know he's getting married to you. Talk about leaving a girl out in the cold."

Only Dee Dee could say something like that, basically put Sara on the spot, and not have it come across as ignorant.

Sean had told Dee Dee on many occasions that it had been a misunderstanding. He had meant it hypothetically. "I never mean to hurt—"

Dee Dee waved a hand to dismiss his effort at an apology.

"I've got a man these days. It's a steady thing, too. Not sure if it's happily-ever-after, but it's going good for now. I'm hearing a lot about you two through the rumor mill and the media. As for the rumor mill, I'm referring to the department."

He breathed a little easier knowing she had someone

in her life. “You might have heard that we opened up a PI firm then.”

“I did, and I assume that has something to do with why you’re here.”

“Your assumption would be correct.” Sean gestured to Sara and she pulled out the baggie of beans.

Chapter 12

Hoping for Answers

Sara handed the bag of coffee beans to Dee Dee. "We need your help to see if these are poisoned."

Dee Dee held it up, studied the contents through the clear plastic. "Poisoned?"

"Yes, and we figured you could help us."

Sara's tone broke many a resolve, so if Dee Dee hadn't planned on helping them, they stood a better chance now.

"You're thinking someone poisoned the coffee?"

"Yes, with cyanide."

"What kind of a sick person would do something like that?"

"That's what we need to figure out. We just need you to—" Sean stopped talking when Dee Dee leveled her gaze on him.

She gave the bag back to Sara, who reluctantly took it. "You're not going to help us because Sean broke your date?"

It wasn't a date. Sean managed to keep his mouth quiet, but he was ready to intercept if the need arose and, based on the volatile energy in the room, that might be sooner than later.

Dee Dee's facial features hardened and her mouth fell in a straight line. "I'm not going to help you because it's something you could just as easily do yourself. Not to mention I have a lot already on the go. You both know what it's like to work for the city. There's more to do in a day than eight hours will allow."

Sean remembered what it was like to have a caseload more comprehensive than the time allowed for thorough investigation. This was something that he was able to conjure up after being away from the job for more than a year. But he also realized why he had put up with it for so long—besides being able to afford food and shelter. He was making a difference by bringing killers to justice and answers to victims' families.

"We will pay the city for your time," he said.

Given the way Dee Dee's expression slipped further, it was the wrong thing to say.

"He didn't mean that the way it came out. We understand you're busy. We're sorry to have bothered you. Come on, darling." Sara tugged on his arm and they both turned around when Dee Dee spoke.

"Wait."

Sean didn't want to get his hopes up, but it was too late for that. He was already getting emotionally involved with this case and it was just starting out. It was an unusual response from him. Typically he preferred the facts to be verified. It must have to do with knowing what it was like to lose two parents. While it was true his weren't stolen from him through murderous hands, he was well aware of the marrow-deep pain that parental loss incurred. It was these thoughts that must have muddled his thinking process earlier.

"You didn't ask how to test them yourself." Dee Dee curled her lips. "Wow, it slipped right over your heads. I can't believe it."

"Neither can I." Sara glanced at Sean.

This was exactly what he was going to bring up, but if he said so now he wouldn't appear credible. "And how can we do that?"

"You said cyanide, right?"

Sara nodded.

"There are places online that will send you strips for testing this sort of thing. You might have to buy them in bulk, but with your money, I don't think it's an issue." She winked at him. Seemingly, any insult she wanted to take to his offer for payment was now behind them. Dee Dee's moods fluctuated like an elevator—up and down.

Chapter 13

Alfalfa Sprouts Bribery

Jimmy stopped outside of the morgue doors and adjusted the lay of his tie while balancing his hold on the sandwich bag. His palms were moist. Why was he letting Needham get to him like this? He had nothing to prove to him. This was ridiculous. He was here for one purpose and then he'd leave. It didn't need to be complicated. Certainly he was blowing it out of proportion in his mind…but that's where his reassurance fell flat. To ask if Needham remembered something from the autopsy implied he had failed to note it in the record. It was this insinuation that made the interaction potentially explosive.

No time like the present.

A well-known phrase that had him straightening his back and pushing through the swinging door.

It met with Albert Needham's nose.

Needham yelped and when he laid his eyes on Jimmy, his nostrils flared. It must have caused another rush of pain as Needham tenderly pressed his fingers to the flesh.

"What are you doing here?"

Jimmy was doing his best to compose himself. It had to be his nerves, but he found the situation funny. Here he was, all worried about seeing the man, building up a confrontation in his head—

"I said, what are you doing here?" Needham ambled

over to his desk in the corner and pulled a tissue from the box. He dabbed his nose while keeping an eye on Jimmy. "Be happy it's not bleeding."

Jimmy ignored the rant. "I brought you lunch."

Needham snatched the bag and deposited it on his desk.

"It's your favorite. Swiss on rye with alfalfa sprouts."

The eye contact held steady.

"I was hoping you had a few minutes."

"You've got one."

The utter disregard for Jimmy's offering was one thing, but it was the tone in Needham's voice that put Jimmy over the edge. No one had the right to speak to another person in this manner. "Out of respect for our time, I will do my best to be quick."

Needham tossed the tissue into the trash can next to his desk and wiped his hands together. "Go ahead."

"You conducted an autopsy two weeks ago on a woman named Beverly Sparks."

"Yes, I remember her. Respiratory failure."

Jimmy wasn't sure whether the sharp memory of the medical examiner was worrisome or provided hope. It could go either way. One, Needham would be insulted by the questioning, or two, with the procedure clear in his mind it might provoke a sensory memory. There was only one way to find out.

"Her daughter believes she was poisoned."

"I remember her carrying on about it, but if her mother was, no evidence supported that in my findings. I can only catalog what I find."

This is where things might get dicey. Jimmy had to push a little. "When you were conducting the autopsy did you notice any odor coming off the body?"

"You mean besides regular decomposition? If there

was anything else, it was masked. What are you driving at? What poison?"

"Cyanide."

"Ah, a bitter-almond smell, but it only results sometimes. Ms. Sparks was dead for twelve hours before she was found, and longer still before she made it to a cooler, let alone my slab."

And there it was, the old man's seeming disregard for the dead. It was a good thing they were incapable of hearing how he spoke about them. Although, maybe they did and haunted him. It could be restless spirits and the resultant lack of a good night's sleep that made the man cantankerous.

"All right. Well, thank you for your help."

"You're welcome."

"Enjoy the sandwich," Jimmy mumbled once his back was turned.

Chapter 14

Good Disguise

"We don't have the time to wait on them to ship out." Sara made a plea to Dee Dee.

"Well, even if I did take on this job for you, I wouldn't be able to get to it right away. I've probably taken up too much time talking to you guys already as it is."

"It's a good thing you're head of this department then." Sean tried to appeal to her ego.

"I still report to people. I'll probably just skip lunch. Eat a carrot stick or something."

Sean wasn't going to touch that. "I'm sure you could use your power of influence and get the strips expedited overnight. If you reach the company before one, you might even have them as soon as tomorrow."

"Can we have the company's name?" Sara asked.

"Sure." Dee Dee walked around behind her desk, opened a drawer, and came out with a business card. She took a pen from the holder and scribbled on the back. "I think their website is their company name with dot net."

Sara touched the back of the woman's hand in the transfer of the card. "Thank you. We appreciate your help."

"I'm sorry I couldn't test them for you. But like I said, time just won't allow for it and especially not as fast as you want results. Now, you said that someone poisoned coffee? I would think the person tasted that it was off."

"It was dark cherry almond flavor," Sean said.

"All right. That I can understand. See, cyanide has an almond-like flavor, but it has a bitter aftertaste. Given the coffee you mentioned they may have thought it was an edge to the beverage. It would be an excellent way to hide the poison. The thing with cyanide is, it has to be in large doses to kill. Either that or prolonged exposure."

"For our case, it was the latter. The victim drank five to six cups a day."

"A day? Speaking of, are you still drinking coffee like that, Sara?"

"How did you—"

Sean cupped his wife's elbow, prodding her to show restraint. The last thing they needed was her getting defensive about her habit, and Dee Dee clamming up as a result. But Sean was curious about one more thing.

"Where do people get cyanide?"

Dee Dee dragged her gaze from Sara to Sean. "First of all, it's not as easy to get as one might think."

Sean took a seat, but, based on the reflection in Dee Dee's eyes, he stood up again.

Dee Dee continued. "Cyanide is released from natural substances such as fruit seeds, apricots, peaches, and apples. Still, the amount required to kill is hard to obtain. In laboratories, it is locked up. It can come in the form of gas, liquid, or white crystal powder. It has practical use in many industrial processes. You said that the coffee was poisoned. Are you thinking this is happening at the company itself?"

"It's too early to know for sure."

"Well, it's probably someone who has easy access to the poison. Maybe a spouse or friend who has a tie to one of the industries that use it. That might be a quick way of narrowing in on whoever did this."

Sean nodded and glanced at Sara.

The clock on Dee Dee's wall was reading just past twelve. They needed to get to a computer and a phone to order those testing strips.

"We better let you get back to things. Thank you, again, for all your help."

"You got it, sweet cheeks." Dee Dee laughed once Sara did.

Chapter 15

That's a Lot of Poison

"See, there were no hard feelings there, Sean." Sara giggled most of the way back to the car.

"You are finding all of this too funny."

"Come on, Sean, don't be so serious. I don't blame her for having a crush on you."

He tapped her nose with his finger. "You are good at charming people you know."

She smiled and sauntered to her side of the car. "One of my gifts, I suppose."

He opened the door for her. "You don't have to suppose—it is."

"Thank you." She was laughing again when he shut her door.

By the time he was behind the wheel, she had composed herself, her mind now on the case. "Sean, if someone at the company poisoned the beans, and it wasn't an intentional effort to kill Beverly, then this is something huge. The person we're after could be responsible for more than one death. If nothing else, their intent was to hurt people. It doesn't matter if their motive was sabotage. The result is the same."

"I know. This case has the potential to be a big one for sure."

"Monumental." She didn't want to admit to Sean that she was thinking about the media attention their agency would get as a result of all this, and the ensuing workload. Dee Dee and her government job would hold no contest when compared to their to-do list.

"We also have the chance to make a difference with this one and save who knows how many others."

"You're right." She'd choose to focus on that aspect as it was more motivating than a busier schedule. She leaned against the headrest. "Dee Dee said the cyanide testing was easy. I wonder why Sophie didn't do it for herself. Or send the beans away?"

"She probably couldn't afford to. We might have to buy the strips in bulk, remember?"

"Of course I remember."

He licked his lips. He was teasing her. Her memory was flawless.

"I don't know. It's likely nothing."

"What is it?"

"Well, she can afford to pay us but she can't afford some strips?"

"We don't even know how much they cost yet." Sean pulled out his smartphone and started moving around the screen. She saw him bring up the Internet browser. "What's the company name again?"

"Pole-Carron, with a hyphen."

"Hmm."

"What is it, Sean?"

"I did a search with the company name and added cyanide test strips. I got to the order page right away."

"And?"

"It's a very small investment. For one hundred strips, it's only a hundred and twenty-five dollars."

Sara hadn't expected that result. Even though her trust was misplaced on occasion, she preferred to give people the benefit of the doubt. It was a happier existence that way. "Maybe she didn't know what she'd do with a hundred of them. But I also remember her saying she didn't know where to test them. Maybe she's not computer savvy." The statement fell from her lips, and she identified it as a flimsy defense. "Never mind. I heard what I said. It doesn't make sense."

They held eye contact for a while with neither of them saying anything.

Sean spoke first. "Before we get too carried away, let's get these beans tested."

Chapter 16

Mulling it Over

It was the next day and Sara was feeling disheartened. She didn't get much sleep because she'd tossed and turned, thinking about Sophie and her mother. The answers weren't coming quickly. And Jimmy hadn't had any luck with Albert Needham. On a good note, the test strips were set to arrive at the firm early that morning.

They also made a call to Adam yesterday to have him research Tasty Beans and to pull an employee list. He had a gift that enabled him to do things behind the scenes. Maybe they weren't always legal, per se, but his skillset served their purposes quite well. The secret was not getting caught. Either way, Sara found it justifiable if it meant the killer answered for his crime.

While Sara had tried to get some words into her manuscript before they were to head over to the office, the creative flow wasn't happening. She had never been one of those authors who pounded out fifteen hundred words an hour, but normally she had something to show for her efforts. So after stumbling through the compilation of three paragraphs, she headed to the front door where she waited for Sean.

"Are you all right?" he asked.

"I've been waiting for a while now."

"Waiting on me? Well, that's a switch." He wrapped his arm around her waist and guided her out of the house.

On the drive, she kept glancing over at him, but his focus was on the road—where it should be really. She reached out and ran her fingers through his hair and tucked some longer strands behind his ear. Not that they were sticking out. Sean always had himself put together—it was one of the things she loved about him. She was simply showing him affection.

He caught her hand and kissed the back of it. "A penny for your thoughts."

"They are more expensive than that." She smiled at him as she pulled her hand back. "Is it just me, or was it easier to separate yourself when you were a cop?"

"I hear what you're saying, darling, I do."

"So you think you get more emotionally involved now, too?"

"I think it's bound to happen. It's our names now. We want to make a difference."

"And you know what? We are, Sean."

"We are." He pointed at the delivery truck in front of the firm. "Looks like we arrived right on time."

Chapter 17

A Sacrifice for the Cause

They were willing to sacrifice the coffee machine for the purpose of this experiment. It was the kind that ground the beans and then brewed the pot. Its value would be added to the expense list for the case if the test strips returned positive.

The motor whirred as it minced the beans, releasing their rich aroma into the air.

"It smells good in here." Helen came from the front and entered the break room. "What is that? Cherry? Almond?"

"Don't get too excited. This is the batch we're testing for cyanide," Sean said.

Helen winced. "I've suddenly lost my urge for a cup."

"Good idea. I wouldn't even recommend inhaling too deeply." He caught the fear in Sara's eyes. "Remember how much Beverly had to drink. If these beans are poisoned, there isn't a high concentration."

"You'd be hoping so anyway, or the three of us will be joining Mrs. Sparks," Sara responded.

Five minutes later they had a half pot of coffee made and Helen had returned to the front desk.

"Moment of truth." Sara turned to Sean, who pulled out one of the strips.

"Now according to the directions, it's an easy process." He held the strip over the coffee and was about to put it in.

"Wait a minute."

His hand stopped, hovering above the brew. "What is it?"

She giggled. "You read directions?"

"Listen, you, I'll deal with you later."

"You'd be thinking so anyway," she teased further. "I'm sorry, go ahead. You know how I sometimes get when I'm nervous."

"Yes, dear. So, according to the directions, we just have to dip this in the liquid, remove it and compare it to this chart they gave us. It takes anywhere from one to ten minutes for the results to show."

"Why do I have a feeling that time will pass slowly?"

"You know what they say about a watched kettle. In this case—"

She held up her hand. "I get it."

About two minutes later, the strip was changing color and a quick comparison with the chart gave them their answer.

"The beans were poisoned," they said in unison.

Chapter 18

Sniffing out a Motive for Murder

Sara hugged Adam when he came into the conference room. "It's good to see you."

"Thanks, I think." Adam passed a glance to Sean.

"So what did you find out for us?" Sean directed Adam to take a seat across from him, next to Jimmy. Sara sat beside Sean.

"I did everything you asked of me and probably more." Adam fired up the laptop and connected wirelessly to the electronic interactive board.

"You'll do anything to show off," Jimmy chirped in.

"Someone has to come to the table. Whoa." Adam laughed.

Jimmy's eyes narrowed. "It's not my fault I got the old coot."

"Come on, Jimmy, he's not that bad," Sara said.

"You're right, he's worse."

Adam logged in to his computer. "I found out the entire history of the company. They are located on the outskirts of Williamsburg, Virginia. Tasty Beans has been in business eighteen years and is a family owned business, a husband and wife team. They have two children—a boy and girl—the 'million dollar family.' The eldest is the son, and he has shares in the company already at the age of sixteen. The daughter will get a portion on her sixteenth birthday, which is still four years away."

"How much is the company worth?"

"They are in the black if you were wondering about them possibly sabotaging themselves as some sort of fraudulent play."

"Continue."

"All right, I'm almost there." With a flick of his wrist, the board lit up with a picture of a family. "These are the McAllisters. The owners, in case you hadn't guessed that already. The husband, Luke, is worth twenty-five million."

"That would be a lot of coffee."

"Yes it would, but they are moving a lot." Adam clicked on the laptop's touchpad. The screen changed. "These are the comparative sales numbers, showing this past fiscal year and five years ago. As you can see, they have grown steadily."

"What about their criminal background?"

"Sean, all of their records are clean."

"It could be one of their employees then. Someone who isn't happy or has a bad history," Sara brainstormed.

"I wasn't able to check into everyone's background. They have more than a couple hundred employees."

Sean let out a whistle. "Coffee is big business."

"You're spot on with that assessment." He gestured with a bob of his head toward the screen. "As you can see, they made twenty-eight million in sales last year alone."

"What about their competition?" Sara asked.

"I was just getting to that. Java Worldwide is their top competitor. They are located in Texas."

"Texas?" Sara chuckled. "I'm not sure why I find that funny, but I just don't think of Texas as coffee land."

"Same with Williamsburg, isn't it?"

"Not as much of a stretch really."

Adam drew his eyes from Sara. "Anyway," he clicked the mouse again and other financials came up, "these are the numbers for JW."

"JW?" Sean asked.

"Java Worldwide."

"Yes, but why abbreviate it?"

Adam shrugged his shoulders. "Does it matter? Anyway, JW is suffering. Their sales are decreasing. I'm thinking it's their motto that is killing them. They promise to deliver worldwide, but they can't control customs and there are delays. It's resulted in an onslaught of horrible customer feedback, and people don't return."

"It's possible that someone from JW is sabotaging TB—What? If you're going to condense one company's name, it's fair game." Jimmy seemed pleased with himself. It caused Sean to smile.

"It is, but remember the distance between them."

"The world is small these days, Adam." This was from Sara. "JW could have placed a corporate spy at Tasty Beans. Only, instead of just observing, they are paid to destroy the company."

"I like the way you think, darling."

"Thank you." She squeezed Sean's hand.

He noticed the two men across from them shaking their heads and making kissy faces at each other to mock him and Sara.

"You guys are just jealous."

"Yeah, the rest of the world is." Adam laughed.

"Not me, not anymore."

"Jimmy?" Sara said slyly.

"Yep, I'm a one-woman man and Meredith has changed my outlook on life."

Adam slapped Jimmy's shoulder. "That's good for you, old man."

"Hey, young whippersnapper."

They all laughed for a few seconds. Sean was the first to return to the serious matter at hand. "Adam, we need you to see if there's any connection between the two companies. Any employees that relocated."

"Remember how I said I did everything you asked of me and probably more? This is the probably more." He clicked the touchpad again, and a picture of a young man filled the screen. He was nondescript in appearance. Brown eyes, brown hair, nothing stood out about him. "Meet Casey Park. He's thirty-five and hungry."

"Hungry?" Jimmy snorted at Adam's word choice.

"As in, for advancement. I was able to pull his financials."

"You're breaking all sorts of laws, aren't you?"

Adam drew his attention from the screen to Jimmy. "I'm innovative."

"Uh-huh."

"Anyway, this guy was on salary at JW for forty-five grand. Less than a year before that he had started out at twenty-two. But get this? He left the company in November."

"So he over-doubled his wage in twelve months and then quit?" Sean asked.

"I'm not sure about that. Now, he started working for Tasty Beans in December. His wage? Thirty-five and they never paid him for the transfer. No moving costs, nothing."

"It is strange that he'd give up his paid holidays at Christmastime to start a new job where he'd get nothing. What do you think, Sean?" Sara asked.

"I find it strange he'd take such a huge cut in pay to relocate from Texas to Williamsburg."

"Except he didn't go without," Adam replied.

"Without what?" Sean asked.

"Compensation. According to his bank records, ten thousand was wired into his account in November and another payment was deposited in December. From January until now, he's received a subsidiary income of five grand a month. I haven't been able to track down its source yet."

Chapter 19

There's a Spy Among Us

Jimmy slouched back into his chair. "The guy is a corporate spy."

"If he is, Java Worldwide isn't doing too good a job covering their tracks," Sean concluded.

"Maybe they didn't think anyone would be interested in the coffee business?"

"Jimmy, globally, it's worth a hundred billion, second only to crude oil." Leave it up to Adam to have the facts.

Sara stood and paced the length of the table. "I think this guy is worth our attention. We need to find out where that money is coming from. You did say the supplemental income was untraceable."

"Within the time constraints I had, yes." Adam's pang of disappointment at reaching these confines was etched in his eyes. "I can definitely look into it further."

"Do that, Adam."

"Sure, Sara."

She stopped walking behind Sean and put her hands on his shoulders. "We need to go to Williamsburg. There's no way around it."

Sean leaned back. "They do say 'Virginia is for lovers.'"

Jimmy smacked his lips. "Will you two cut it out or get a room?"

"Don't hate us because we're beautiful, rich, and in love," Sean replied.

"You had to throw in all three, didn't you?" Jimmy let a few seconds pass before speaking again. "What are you going to do once you get there? It's not like you can just walk in the front door and start asking questions."

It had Sara thinking about their PI licenses and, in a case like this, they were almost useless. While they were afforded access to databases for background information on people, the state of Virginia didn't have a reciprocity agreement with the state of New York. In fact, New York State didn't have one with any of the other states. That meant they were limited when it came to presenting themselves as investigators. And even if they could go in spouting off questions, the killer wasn't going to willingly come forward. "We'll have to act like regular citizens."

"You're probably right. We can't just walk in there and speak with Casey Park."

"We could always talk to him at home."

Sean bobbed his head side to side. "That's an option. Adam, what does Casey do for Tasty Beans?"

"He's in the flavoring oils department."

"So, let me sum this up. He transferred from Texas to Virginia for a loss in wage. He's receiving money each month from an unknown source. And now you're telling me he works in the department responsible for adding the flavor to the beans?"

"You got it, Sara."

"Call the pilot, Sean. We're going to meet Casey Park in person. Jimmy, we need you on standby. Adam, dig deeper with those bank deposits. Find their source."

"I'm on it."

Chapter 20

Wigs and Mustaches

Their private jet touched down at Williamsburg Airport just after one in the afternoon. The fact they could take off at a moment's notice to anywhere in the world still came as a rush to Sean. He didn't see it ever growing old.

Adam had obtained Casey's working hours and discovered he pulled the afternoon shift, from three until eleven. It didn't leave them much time to get over to his house for a chat.

"Are you sure I look good as a blonde?" Sara was studying her reflection in the vanity mirror of the Toyota they had rented. She adjusted the wig and swiped a longer strand from her eyes.

"You're a heartbreaker regardless of your hair color, darling."

She laughed. "You're just saying that because you want some. I know you."

"Can't blame a guy."

"Oh, I can and I will. And this makeup? Too much? It is, isn't it?"

He glanced over at her but didn't say anything. When they decided to come to Virginia to talk to Casey, Helen had suggested they needed disguises.

She had said, "You're like gossip-rag celebs now."

"Gossip rag?" He hadn't been sure whether to be complimented by that or not.

Helen had smiled. "You don't need to take offense. Your faces are just well known. You've been on TV, and in magazines, newspapers. You probably have sites dedicated to following your lives by now. I'm surprised paparazzi aren't camped outside."

"Now you're taking it a little far."

"The point is, you can't go there without some sort of a disguise." Helen had then got to work on him and Sara.

Sean had barely recognized his reflection by the time she was finished with him. The only things that remained true were his eyes. He saw himself there, but everywhere else, well, not so much.

Helen had had Adam going one direction and Jimmy going another. While Adam hit the thrift stores, Jimmy had bought wigs and makeup. Her motherly attributes were obvious, the way she'd had the men jumping to her direction.

"Sean, are you listening to me?"

He realized Sara was waiting for an answer. "Sorry, darling, I was just thinking."

"Don't be sorry for that."

Sara ran a fingertip around her mouth, likely trying to rein in the bright red lipstick from taking over her face.

"Be happy you don't look like a seventies pop star," he said.

Jimmy had found two wigs. He'd been ever-so-helpful, and Sean intended to repay him for that. One wig for Sara would have been enough. Why did he need one too? As it turned out, he was wearing a hairpiece that had a ponytail at the nape of his neck—an "added touch" by the lovely Helen—but he wore a fake mustache.

"I can't believe you're complaining. You resemble Magnum now." She laughed. "And you have the license."

"Ha ha." A conversation from not so long ago was back to haunt him. He'd have to start considering the long-term ramifications of anything he was inclined to say from now on. Apparently their hang-time was perpetual.

"At least you get to remain a brunet."

"I hear that blondes have more fun."

"We'll see about that."

Chapter 21

"Won't You Be My Neighbor"

Sean rang Casey's doorbell and Sara swayed from side to side. Her skirt, a find that Adam had made at a thrift shop, was definitely not something she would have considered, even before she was a billionaire. Its length was below her knees but flared out like a fifties-style poodle skirt, and it was bright red. It matched the shade of lipstick she wore. Even though she'd never dress like this for real, it was kind of fun. It was like Halloween in May.

As she clasped her hands behind her back, she studied her husband's garb. She stifled the laughter, but it wasn't easy.

"What, Miss Mayberry?"

"You're one to talk. ABBA's missing a singer."

He was dressed in tight, white bell-bottoms and a gold puffy-sleeved shirt. The ensemble was suitable for platform shoes, but that's where he had drawn the line.

"You play mean."

She couldn't help it now. She laughed.

Sara wasn't sure what either of them were thinking—if they were—when they agreed to these elaborate costumes. But one thing was certain, they didn't resemble their real selves at all. She just didn't know why they had to look like they were from another decade to do it. Oh well. It was all for a good cause.

The door opened and it was Casey. "What can I do

for—" He stopped talking as he took in their outfits.

"We live just down thataway." Sara pointed down the street, in no particular direction. "We just like to meet our neighbors. May we come in?" Sara asked, laying on all the charm. Without the getup, Casey would have stepped aside already. As it was now, he barred entry.

"Listen, I've gotta get ready for work."

"Oh, don't let us stop you, sugar." Sugar? She glanced at Sean. His mouth was twitching like he was trying to suppress a smile. "We'll only take but a minute of your time." She squeezed between Casey and the doorframe.

"What do you think you're doing?"

"Just a little chitchat, 'kay, neighbor?"

Casey opened the door to allow Sean in.

"First off, what's your name?"

"Casey."

"That's a real nice name."

"Thanks."

Sara wandered a bit inside his townhouse. The main entry wasn't very big. There was a hallway that led to a back room and stairs off to the immediate right. She pointed upward. "This the way to your sitting area?" She took the first few steps without waiting for an answer.

Growing up, her girlfriend had lived in a townhouse like this one and they were all fashioned the same way. The entry level had laundry and a rec room, the first had the kitchen and living room and from there, a staircase led to the top floor where the bathroom and bedrooms were.

"I don't know who you two are, but I've got to get ready for work. If you could please—" Casey gestured back toward the door.

"Oh, don't be silly." Sean laid a hand on his shoulder.

"A man always has time for his neighbors."

Sara heard Sean's feet on the steps. Casey sighed but resigned to following them. Of course, with complete strangers in his home he didn't have much choice.

Chapter 22

False Identities

Sara dropped onto Casey's sofa and Sean sat beside her.

"By all means, make yourselves comfortable." Casey flailed his arms in the air.

She flashed a smile, keeping in mind that Sean had told her it had the ability to disarm any man's resolve. She was also a brunette at the time.

"Coffee? Tea? Water?" Casey asked.

"No, thank you. You, darlin'?" She turned to Sean.

"Nope."

"All right." Casey thumped down into a ratty recliner but didn't bother to crank up the leg rest. "What did you two say your names were?"

"Well…we didn't." Sara faced Sean.

"Why, we're…" Sean met her eyes.

Her mind went blank. It was just like earlier that morning when she'd tried to write. Even when she was in a groove, assigning names to secondary characters was sometimes a difficult accomplishment.

"This here is Gwen, my wife, and I'm Stephan."

Her eyes widened. She was certain her mouth gaped open a bit too.

"Gwen and Stephan? Kind of like that singer."

Sara waved her hand to dismiss the comment. "Yeah, sort of like that."

Casey glanced away for a second and that's all it took

for her to fire a glare to Sean.

"What?" he mouthed with a tight jaw.

"So." Casey ran his hands down his thighs.

"We've been wanting to get over here to meet you for a while." Sara crossed her legs and clasped her hands on her kneecap. "Ya moved here in—what?—January?"

"November, but that's close."

"Cool, cool. And where were ya before that?"

"I'm not sure if I'm comfortable with all the questions."

"Yeah, I guess we are basically strangers," Sean said.

"Don't be silly, Se—" She almost messed up. "Stephan, darlin'. We're neighbors." She offered Casey a cheesy grin. "So where was that?" She hitched up her brows to emphasize the question.

"Texas."

"Oh, the Lone Star State. Everyone has a gun out there."

"Yes they do."

"Do you still have one?"

"I might."

"That's a long move. Why here?"

"Work."

This process was painfully tedious. Casey was definitely a reserved individual. Whether it was because he had something to hide or not remained to be seen. So far they weren't getting anything new. "And what's work?"

"Something I'm going to be late for if I don't get going soon. Listen, it's been real nice meeting you…"

Sara could have detected the lie without his telltale sign. As he spoke, he tugged on an earlobe.

"No harm in telling us where you work. I work at Tasty Beans."

Casey's eyes—and Sean's—snapped to her.

"Yep, that's right. I start tomorrow on the evenin' shift."

"That's quite the coincidence."

"Nah, shucks, you work there too?"

"I do."

"Well, Stephan here is trying to get in too. Maybe you could put in a good word for him, seeing as you've been there longer."

Casey stood. "Ah, yeah, sure. I'll see what I can do."

"Just wonderful." Sara clapped her hands and stood. "We'll see ourselves out. It was real nice meeting ya."

"Yep."

Sara sensed his eyes on their backs as they walked away. She glanced into the kitchen and spotted a bowl of apples on the counter. Dee Dee had said that cyanide was found in their seeds. She stopped moving and turned around.

"Actually, if you're still offering, I'd like a glass of milk. I can help myself."

"Sure, why not?"

The exasperation in his voice carried the unspoken words, *you're going to do what you like anyway.*

She hated drinking milk by itself, but it was the only way she could get into his fridge. She was taking a bet on whether the single man would have milk, but the wager had paid off.

"The glasses?" She drew her finger along the wall of cabinets.

Casey took a glass from the cabinet closest to the fridge. "Here."

"Why, thank you ever so much." Sara opened the door and spotted the carton right away, but she was more interested in the number of apples in the crisper. She wasn't sure whether to comment on it, but if this was their killer, she couldn't risk tipping him off. Not to mention, the fact that he had a gun was still clear in her mind.

She closed the fridge door without getting milk. She extended the empty glass back to Casey. "On second thought, too much milk isn't good for a girl's waistline. Ta-ta. Maybe I'll see you at Tasty Beans tomorrow."

"You never know. I could be lucky."

Sara's intuition took that statement to mean if he was lucky he wouldn't. It had to be the blond wig.

Chapter 23

Improvisation

They headed back to the rental car, which they had parked down the street to add some credence to their cover story about being Casey's neighbors. They didn't need him to see them loading into the vehicle out front of his house.

Sean had walked around to open Sara's door. She faced him. "Okay, you couldn't do any better than Gwen and Stephan?"

"Excuse me, you're the writer and nothing was coming from you. I had to think fast."

"Hmm." She got in.

"And you work at Tasty Beans?" he asked as he slipped behind the wheel.

"I think we both do. There's no way he's going to open up to us as neighbors."

He stopped short of turning the key in the ignition. "No, no, no. Don't drag me into this."

"Listen, we have to do what we have to do to solve this thing, Sean. One woman has already died. How many more out there are sick and in danger of losing their lives? We have to stop this thing right now."

"All right, and how do you intend to arrange employment?"

"I have a little arsenal in my pocket. His name is Adam." She pulled out her cell phone and put him on speaker. "Go ahead," she said to Sean.

"How are you coming with tracing those deposits to Casey's bank account?"

She whispered to Sean, "That's not the question I called him about."

He shrugged his shoulders and in a low voice said, "You should have started the conversation then."

Her face fell. There was no retort for that. He had a point.

"Unfortunately, nowhere with it yet, and it's not for a lack of trying. I will keep on it."

The line went silent and Sara realized that Sean was leaving this up to her. If she wanted them to work for Tasty Beans, she'd have to get it arranged.

"There's something else we need your help with," she began.

"Anything."

She hesitated, only briefly. "We need you to get us jobs at Tasty Beans."

"Jobs? I am hearing you right?"

"You are. It's the only way we can get close enough to figure out what's going on."

"I assume you met Casey and he didn't offer much?"

"Your assumption's correct. It doesn't seem I wield as much power as a blonde."

"I highly doubt that."

"Adam," Sean blurted out.

"Sorry, Mr. McKinley. I didn't mean anything by it. It's just that—"

"I understand. So, can you get us in? Not that I really want in." He whispered the last part to Sara.

"Jobs at Tasty Beans? I'll see what I can do. I assume you'd ideally like to be near Casey Park and on his shift."

"Yes, ideally."

"All right, I'll see what I can do."

"One more thing."

"Yes, Sean."

Sean sliced a glance to Sara but spoke to Adam. "If we're going to be working there, we'll need to know how the company operates, the manufacturing processes involved in flavoring beans and shipping them out."

"You got it."

"I'll pass that task to Helen if you don't mind, and I'll keep on the money transfers and getting you employment."

"Sounds like a good idea."

Sara witnessed the reflection in Sean's eyes. He had another revelation but was debating whether or not to verbalize it. Seconds later, he did.

"Make sure you get us in different departments so we can get a good feel for everything and are able to talk to more people."

"Anything else?"

"Two things, our names are Gwen and Stephan Levine." Sean spoke over Adam's laughter. "And get Jimmy down here."

"What?" Sara mouthed as she touched Sean's arm. "And Levine? I guess we're sticking with the music industry theme."

Sean smiled at her. "Get him a job, too. Make it in the shipping department. We don't know at what point the poison is being added to the beans. We're assuming it's Casey in flavoring, but we need to cover all angles."

"I'll see what I can do on that, but I'll tell him to get his bags packed."

"Good job. As soon as we get settled into a hotel, we'll let you know where we are. I'll call the pilot once we hang up here. Tell Jimmy to be ready for a seven o'clock flight. We'll also get him a room."

"You got it."

Sean ended the call. "I hope you're happy, Sara."

"What did I do?"

"You are dragging poor Jimmy down here."

"Hey, that part was all you. Besides, a little hard work never hurt anyone. And Jimmy's good at talking people up. If anyone can get drivers to talk, it's him. Still, I have a feeling you might regret this."

He turned the car on, put it into gear, and reached for her hand. "You don't have to have a feeling about it, I already do. But, while we're in Virginia, let's make the best of it, shall we, darling."

"And your mind's in the gutter again."

"What do you mean *again*?" He winked at her.

Chapter 24

Checking In

Sean tracked down a nice hotel and they secured two rooms—one for them and one for Jimmy. At first, the people at the front desk treated them like riffraff, but when the platinum plastic came out and their identification was confirmed, the hotel staff was eager to please.

"Mr. and Mrs. McKinley, we are honored you are staying at our hotel." The hotel manager's eyes assessed their appearances. The introductions had already been made. His name was Ruben Holloway. "I must say you both look quite different than you do on TV. You must be undercover for a case. That's it, isn't it? This is exciting."

Sean tucked a few hundred-dollar bills into the man's hand. "We need you and your staff's discretion. You are right, we're on a case, but we need you to keep it quiet."

He shook his mitt full of money at Sean. "You got it. Anything else I can do, Mr. McKinley, let me know personally. Day or night. The front desk has ways of reaching me."

Sean let his eyes drift to Ruben's hand, insinuating the cash he'd just given him should earn them direct access.

"Oh, oh. Yes, of course." Ruben reached inside his suit jacket and pulled out a business card. From the left breast pocket of his shirt, he pulled out a pen. He scribbled on the back of the card and then extended it to Sean. "That is my cell number."

While he was handing the information to Sean, his eyes diverted to Sara. "If it's not improper to say, Mrs. McKinley, blond suits you."

"That's kind of you. Thank you," she said.

"Don't mention it. Now, Leo will get your bags and take them to your room." Ruben snapped his fingers and a man in his early twenties came running.

"Yes, boss."

"Be sure to see these two fine people to their room."

Leo looked at Sean and Sara, his eyes tracing down Sean's bell-bottoms and then Sara's skirt.

"Leo?" The manager snapped his fingers again.

"Yes, right this way."

It was refreshing that Leo seemed to have no idea who they were. Apparently their true identities meant nothing among the twenty-year-old demographic. All this guy noticed was what he could physically see before him and nothing beyond that. He was probably wondering how a couple who dressed as they did could afford the nightly rate at this hotel.

Chapter 25

Magnum's off the Table

Sean called Adam from their room to let him know where they were and that Jimmy would just need to show his ID at the front desk. "There's no need for him to see us when he gets here. Tell him there's a morning breakfast buffet and we'll meet him in the restaurant around seven."

"Will do. Have a good night."

"You too." Sean put his phone on the nightstand. "There we have it, darling. All alone for the night. In Virginia. The place for lovers."

Sara laughed. "Would you cut it out? You're wearing that one out."

"Fine then." He pretended his ego was bruised, but it would take a lot more than that.

They got to work taking off all the layers that had identified them with their alter egos, Gwen and Stephan, except Sean left the mustache in place.

Dinner was brought to the room, and afterward they got on the bed to talk as the chairs at the table were not designed for comfort. Neither was the couch, which was surprising for the cost of the room.

Sean grabbed his mustache as if grooming it and then curled back his top lip until it touched his nose. "So, darling, are you sure I can't keep it?"

She put her fingertip to his lips. Her eyes softened as she let her gaze linger on his mouth. He was moving in for a kiss when she pulled back and shot up her hand up between them. "Ah, no, not if you want to kiss me."

"That solves that then. I'm over the thing." He tugged a corner of it and ripped it off with a single swipe. Tears filled his eyes. His nose started to run. He let out a yelp—delayed but nonetheless sincere. That didn't go anything like he'd seen it in his mind. It was supposed to come off effortlessly and fly across the room. Then he was going to capture his wife in his arms and make love to her.

"Oh, Sean." Sara positioned herself on her knees and touched the top of his lip that was now bare but likely a glowing red.

"Please, don't—" Even the subtle brush of her fingertips caused another wave of agony to surge through him.

She dropped her hands. "Sorry."

He shook his head. He was in too much pain to form words just yet. Seconds ticked by, maybe an entire minute, before the stinging receded enough to gather his voice.

"I don't think I'll be getting that back on tomorrow."

She cupped his cheek in her hand, sticking to the outside of his face and away from his nose. "We can just say you shaved it off if Casey notices."

"We're going to have to."

"So if you get to lose the 'stache, can I drop the wig?"

"No way."

Her eyes narrowed. "That's hardly fair."

"Seems to me your wig came off without taking flesh with it so it's not exactly the same thing."

"Speaking of."

"What?"

"Your lip looks so raw now, but there's no blood."

"Thank heaven for small miracles."

She smirked and angled her head to the left. "If it's still red in the morning, we'll have to say that you had an allergic reaction to a new shaving gel you tried."

"Shaving gel? That works for me." He moved up the bed and positioned himself with his back against the headboard. Sara moved with him, but she stayed on her side and let her legs go out toward the middle.

"Do you think Casey is behind this?"

"It's looking good for him."

"It is. And all those apples. What single person needs that many? I mean he's either on an apple diet or he's using the seeds for the cyanide."

"Dee Dee said it would take a lot of them for there to be any effect."

"And you don't consider a large bowl and a crisper full to be a lot?"

"I never said that." He let his thoughts drift. The throbbing in his lip continued on, but the discomfort had died down enough for him to focus his thoughts elsewhere. "Adam told us Casey's in the flavoring department at Tasty Beans. It's quite possible he's behind the poisoning."

"Corporate sabotage." Sara shook her head. "It's just sad that so many are going to have to pay because of greed."

Sean put his arm up, signaling for Sara to come under it and snuggle into him. She followed the cue and, once settled there, put her hand on his chest.

"That's just one reason why I love you, you know."

"What's that, Sean?"

He kissed her forehead. "You care so much about people."

Chapter 26

Undercover Mishap

Jimmy was already on to his second plate of bacon and eggs when he spotted Sean and Sara entering the restaurant—a version of them anyway. As good as it was to see them, he wasn't really looking forward to sharing all of the news he had to convey.

"Good morning, Jimmy." Sara sat across from him.

"How was your flight?" Sean asked.

"Everything was great." He could say that about the travel, even though he hadn't been so fond of getting on the plane at first. It brought back some bad memories, but he had the McKinleys' stewardess bring him a nice glass of Scotch, and his nerves relaxed. There were some things he needed to tell Sean and he had a feeling he wouldn't see them as great. "Hey, what happened to the mustache?"

Sean took a seat across from Jimmy while Sara excused herself to get a cup of coffee.

"Don't even ask."

Jimmy wanted to respond with *too late for that*, but let it go. "So, Sara's still drinking the stuff, I see." Jimmy gestured toward Sara, who was filling her mug with the dark brew.

"I think it would take a little more than poison to make her stop—unfortunately. She claims that it's because the woman drank flavored. Apparently that's where everything went wrong." Sean fiddled with his knife and fork, which sat on a napkin in front of him. "Isn't that coffee?" He pointed to Jimmy's cup.

"Nope, not until we get this case solved. This is Earl Grey tea."

"I never saw you as the type."

"This old man still has some new tricks."

Sara returned with two mugs and set one in front of Sean. "Here you go, darling."

"It's obviously not stopping you," Jimmy pointed out.

"There's no need for paranoia."

Jimmy leaned across the table, passing a furtive glance left and right. "Speaking of, what's to say that only the dark cherry almond flavor was poisoned?"

Sean responded. "Nothing really. It is possible others were."

"Adam's done more digging on the company, and its online feedback forum is getting more complaints about people associating their feeling unwell to the coffee."

"Sean, this is out of hand. How many more will end up like poor Mrs. Sparks?" She was in the process of lifting her cup for a sip but put it back on the table. "Maybe I'll try to go without until I know the company who sold the hotel these beans."

Sean flagged down a busboy who was removing dirty plates from a seating that had just left.

"You want me?" the boy asked.

"Would you know where you get your coffee? It's wonderful."

"I can find out." He threw the last few remaining pieces of cutlery from the table into his bin and walked off.

"You don't have the strips with you?" Sara asked Sean.

"Not that we could use them, in here, in front of

everyone."

"After we hear back from the kid, I'll fill you in on everything," Jimmy said.

"The process of how the beans are flavored would be useful before we start our jobs. Adam did get us jobs right?" Sara asked.

"He did." Jimmy dropped his fork and balled up his napkin.

"What is it?" She cocked her head, adding emphasis to her inquiry.

Sometimes he wished the woman was a little less intuitive, but she had this ability to almost read minds at times. Times like now, specifically.

"We all have jobs."

"Excuse me." The busboy was back, and the three of them turned to him.

He kept his eyes on Sean when he spoke, although his gaze drifted to Sara. She could probably dye her hair a bright purple and still attract men.

"They get their beans from Tasty Beans. It's a local company. Enjoy." With that the kid left them.

"Well, that does it for me." Sean pushed his mug away.

"Me too." Sara followed suit.

She leaned on the table, clasping her hands, her eyes wide with excitement. "Tell us about our jobs."

It was only seven o'clock in the morning. It had to be noon somewhere in the world.

"What is it, Jimmy? You look like you're going to be sick." Sara seemed concerned, the way her facial expression softened, and Sean watched him as if expecting bad news.

"The good part is that the place is large enough that new hires can slip in under the radar. They do their hiring through an employment company. You know, the kind that filter out prospective employees and position temps and the like. Well, Adam was able to hack into their system. We all start on the afternoon shift."

"Wonderful."

Sean shimmied toward Sara. "I'm not sure why you're so excited about having a job."

"It's not that, Sean. It's the fact that we're in and that's the only way we're going to get anywhere with this case. It's the only way we can stop the poisoning and have the killer brought to justice."

"You're right, darling." Sean put his arm around the back of Sara's chair. "Tell us about our jobs."

"Sara's in the flavoring department with Casey. We figured that if anyone could charm the truth out of him it would be her."

Jimmy watched as the first part settled in with Sean.

"So, my wife's working side by side with the killer."

"We don't know that yet, Sean. And you know I can take care of myself."

"You're right. You can." Sean turned back to Jimmy. "And you and I, what are we doing?"

Jimmy wiped his mouth with the napkin. It was a pitiable delay tactic, but whatever worked. He wasn't sure why he dreaded delivering this message when he should have found some pleasure in it. After all, this was the man who'd sent him to speak to Needham—of all people—a couple days ago.

"You're a janitor, and I'm a driver, just like you asked Adam to arrange."

"I'm a what?"

Sara snickered.

"Why am I a janitor?"

Sara's laughter was somewhat contagious, but the

scowl on Sean's face made him restrain himself.

"You asked Adam to put me in as a driver. They only had one other position open."

"A janitor?"

"Yes, Sean."

Sara appeared close to crying from hysteria. Jimmy couldn't fight it anymore and chuckled too.

"I'm glad you two find it so amusing," Sean sulked.

"Come on, darling. You'll be so cute, hauling that mop and bucket along behind you, especially with that nice ponytail of yours."

"I can already picture it," Jimmy managed to get out.

Sean stood. "I'm going to get myself a piece of toast and an egg."

Chapter 27

Withdrawal Jitters

After breakfast, the three of them went up to Sean and Sara's room to go over everything in more detail. Jimmy was briefing them on how beans were flavored, and providing them with an idea of how Tasty Beans was organized.

Sean and Sara were on the sofa and Jimmy was in one of the chairs. He dragged it over so he was closer to them.

Sara didn't really want to verbalize her craving for a robust cup of java, but all this talk about beans wasn't going to help her predicament. If the hotel served coffee from the local company, it was quite likely many in the area would do so as well. But surely there had to be someplace that brought in their coffee from elsewhere. There had to be…

First she'd have to acknowledge her dependency on the beverage to get them out looking for her. And fessing up to her need would equate to a heavy drinker admitting to alcoholism—she'd fall into the addict category. She shook her head at the labels spinning in her mind. Her caffeine enslavement wasn't hurting anyone. Maybe if she became active in the conversation, it would help. "What does Tasty Beans do, exactly?"

"Well, when they get the beans they've already been processed." Jimmy hoisted his one leg over the other and continued. "There are five common roasts—American,

Viennese, Italian, French Dark, and Espresso Black..."

Jimmy kept talking, but she wasn't really listening. All she could think about was a full-bodied coffee coating her palate. She held out her hand. The good news was it wasn't shaking yet.

"—the perfect roast for flavored coffee is medium to dark. And, that's where you'll work next to Casey."

She tucked her hand under her leg, hoping that the men wouldn't have noticed how she had held it out a moment earlier. She needed to come back with something to show her mind was following the conversation. "How is the flavoring added?"

"Two ways. For whole beans, flavoring is added through spraying. For ground beans, it can be mixed in. Before you ask, both methods are used at Tasty Beans."

"Sounds like quite the elaborate process, eh, darling? You probably never thought about how much went into that cup of coffee." Sean reached for her hand. He watched her take it out from under her leg to meet his halfway. It was possible he hadn't caught on to her, but her mind was screaming so loud for a coffee, she just assumed everyone could hear it.

"What else should we know, Jimmy?"

"From there it's sent through quality control. It sits for four days and is then shipped."

Sean let go of her hand and straightened out. "Quality control. You're telling me that people, in-house, are drinking this tampered coffee?"

"It is quite possible."

"Three o'clock can't come fast enough."

Sara glanced at Sean, but she wasn't going to remind him that he'd be picking up a broom at that time. She had her own drama to sort through. How was she going to work in a coffee factory without some caffeine in her system? Surely a chain coffee shop wouldn't risk using someone else's coffee with their name stamped on each cup.

"Guys, why don't we go for a little drive around Williamsburg? We have time for a little sightseeing." What she didn't add was that somewhere along the way she'd be taking them into a Dunkin' Donuts.

Chapter 28

Roll Call

The woman at the front counter of Tasty Beans directed them to follow a security guard. He led them back to a heavy-set woman in human resources who was holed up behind a desk. Her gaze traveled over the three of them.

"Who are they?" she asked the guard.

"New hires sent over from the agency."

The woman rolled her eyes and let out an audible sigh. "Sit them outside there. I'll come get them one at a time."

"You got it." The guard directed them to a row of chairs that lined the wall across from her office. "Take a seat and she'll be out for you soon." He walked off mumbling, not waiting for them to follow his instructions.

Sean couldn't discern what he was saying, but imagined it had something to do with the lady's lack of decorum.

The woman got up and shut her door.

Jimmy leaned in toward Sean. "She's a sweetie pie."

"She's probably not used to three hires showing up at once."

Sara nudged into Sean's side. "Adam would have called, posing on behalf of the agency right? I mean if—"

The door opened again and the woman called out,

"Gwen Levine."

"That's you, darling," Sean said.

Sara got up and went into the office. Sean heard the woman tell her to shut the door. It wasn't long after and Sara came out.

Casey came down the hall toward them. He saw Sean and then did a double-take. "You got a job here after all?"

Sara intercepted and went up to Casey. "He did. We must be the luckiest people in the world."

"Oh yes, lucky."

Sean read the sarcasm in Casey's eyes. He wasn't so certain about their jobs at Tasty Beans denoting luck, but in this economy, getting a job was something to celebrate.

"You're going to take me to my post—I mean, our post?" Sara smiled at Casey, her eyes all doe-like.

Sean realized she was role-playing and winked at her when he was certain Casey wouldn't notice. The guy's gaze went back to him though.

"There's something different about you. Didn't you have a mustache?"

"Sometimes a guy needs to change things up." Sean touched the top of this lip and it was enough to prod the recollection of the pain from the night before. At least his skin wasn't red when he woke up.

"Ah. I guess so."

"Shall we get to work?" This was from Sara, who was still attentive to Casey as if a high school teenager.

"Yeah, sure. Let's get to it."

Sean watched after Sara as she left with Casey. The knight inside of him, the portion of him that required he be Sara's protector, didn't want her to go with him. But she was more than capable of taking care of herself.

He preferred to believe that everything would be fine. It's not like Casey would kill her here anyway…right?

"Gavin Rossdale," the woman bellowed from inside her office. This time she never even bothered to get up. "I said, Gavin Rossdale."

"I think that's you, Jimmy."

"Really, Gavin?"

"Guess so. It is Gwen Stefani's husband's name."

"Does this day get any better?"

"For you it does. I'll be swinging a mop and cleaning out toilet bowls soon enough."

"Point taken. Gavin, it is. I won't say another word about it." Jimmy guffawed as he got up.

Chapter 29

On-The-Job Training

Sara kept pace beside Casey. Just as she had assumed, the smell of coffee beans permeated the building and she was happy that they had found a Dunkin' Donuts. Despite the fact it was now three in the afternoon, and other days she could have easily drunk six coffees by that point, one was enough to keep her from shaking. She used the lack of withdrawal symptoms to soothe any earlier inclinations that she might be an addict. She could cut back her intake.

"So, tell me everything," she said to Casey.

He turned to her and kept walking. "You've never worked for a coffee company before?"

"Nope." She said it with an innocent flair, hoping he'd find her cute, past the blond wig and the fact she was married.

"It's not that hard of a job, but it might be overwhelming at first. We have a quota to meet each shift but don't worry, the beans are in huge mixers." He took them right down another long corridor. "There are three mixers dedicated to our signature flavor alone. You do know what that is?"

She considered playing stupid but didn't see the harm in confirming her knowledge. "Dark cherry almond."

"Right." There was the hint of a smile. He opened a swinging door and held it back for her. "Now, you're going to have to suit up here." He pointed to a dispenser on the wall for white caps. "You'll have to tuck your hair up. Can you imagine what would happen if a customer found hair in their beans?"

While the thought was revolting, Sara's mind thought of one much worse.

SEAN WAITED PATIENTLY FOR JIMMY to finish up with the human resources lady. She took ten minutes with Jimmy and he came out wearing a comical T-shirt with the company's logo center mass.

It only took what seemed like two minutes for Sean to be shown the janitor closet and given a breakdown on what he'd be responsible for from the hours of three to eleven each day.

At the top of the list were the factory bathrooms. It took a lot of self-talk for Sean to give in to the fact he was likely the richest man in the world cleaning public toilets. It was certainly a call to infamy he could have done without. Maybe he could get his job switched around with Jimmy's. But even as the thought entered his mind, it was kicked out. Jimmy was perfect for talking up customers and the other drivers. Even though Casey was their chief suspect, they had to remain open to other possibilities.

Sean would be calling Adam on his first break to prompt him for an update on Casey's financials. Not that Sean was typically a micromanager, but bathrooms? The thought made his stomach roil and his heartburn flare up. It had been a long time since he'd felt that discomfort. Yet here he was, stuck without anything to calm it down, and he was confident that swiping the inside of a toilet bowl was going to make it worse.

Somehow he'd have to place himself out of body.

After dinner break at five, he'd have the offices to do—emptying their trash and cleaning their washrooms. He'd also have to wash all the floors.

According to the schedule, every Friday he would have to vacuum some of the older ones that still had carpeting. It was Tuesday. He hoped the case would be wrapped up by then.

Guess time would tell.

Chapter 30

More Than an Omission

The man approaching Jimmy was dressed in a Tasty Beans T-shirt. It matched the one that Jimmy was told to put on before being directed where to go. Based on the open bay doors and the two delivery trucks backed up to the loading docks, it was apparent Jimmy had the right place. Now he was supposed to seek out a Bruce Baldwin, who was the shipping manager. He had a feeling the man coming toward him was Bruce.

"Who are you?"

"I'm Jim—Gavin Rossdale."

"Which is it, Jim or Gavin?" The man crossed his arms.

Obviously there were a few people at Tasty Beans who didn't much care for their jobs.

"Gavin."

"Well, Gavin, I'm not sure what the agency told you, but there's no position here for you."

"What? I was—"

"Forget what you were told." The man was obviously Bruce, based on his territorial stance.

"But I need this job." Jimmy pretended to panic and it wasn't that hard to conjure up. If he lost his job, Sean would willingly quit to open up a slot in the cleaning department.

"I appreciate that it's a tough economy."

"I'm a hard worker and I know my way around customers. I received a star of excellence from my former employer." All right, so maybe Jimmy was stretching the truth a bit. But if they were going to get to the bottom of what was going on at Tasty Beans, some exceptions needed to be made.

"The star of excellence you say? Well, we could always use the help. Don't misunderstand what I said earlier. I don't know what they told you down at the agency, but this isn't a long-term placement. It will be temporary. Likely very temporary. My name's Bruce Baldwin."

"Nice to meet you."

"Yep, now follow me and I'll introduce you to Luke. He'll be running you through how everything works and getting you out on a truck. You do have your CDL?"

Jimmy recognized the abbreviation as a commercial driver's license. "Of course." This was another lie and could cause damage if he got behind the wheel, but he had no intentions of letting that happen. He'd come up with excuses to get him by for the duration of this ruse.

"I'm going to need to get a copy for the file."

"I gave it to the—" Jimmy stopped talking. He was going to say the agency had it but then the man would go calling over there and they'd have no idea who Gavin Rossdale was—besides Gwen Stefani's husband. "I left it at home."

"That wasn't thinking, now was it?"

"I'm sorry. I didn't think I'd be driving the first day." A lame excuse, but he hoped Bruce would let him have it.

"We'll get you hooked up with Luke and he'll do the driving today." They made it to the shipping office and Bruce grabbed a clipboard off the wall. "Here, hold this." Then he picked up the receiver of a nearby phone and paged over the speaker system. "Luke, to shipping. Luke, to shipping."

And so it began. Jimmy had exchanged his badge for a coffee uniform. He glanced down at the shirt. It was teal with brown ribs that lined the ends of the short sleeves and the scoop of the neck. On the front was a circle with a steaming coffee cup in the middle, but instead of it simply being wisps of white vapor, three sets of beans formed hearts. The company name followed the curve of the circle with Tasty arched at the top and Beans at the bottom. It was more cheerful than he was at the moment. He wondered how Sean and Sara were making out.

Chapter 31

It's All in the Process

Sara analyzed the machine in front of her. It was essentially a trough made of stainless steel. Inside, curved blades came off a center axis and Sara could imagine they spun when the power was turned on. The tub was full of beans and, she assumed, waiting on Casey's return.

"What is this machine?"

"It's called a ribbon blender."

"Ribbon?" She imagined what might result if one fell victim to the metal once it started to spin.

"Yes. Those," he signaled toward the inside of the machine, "are called ribbons. They are not blades if that's what you were thinking. Although, I still wouldn't recommend getting your arm caught up in there."

The way he spoke of getting 'caught up' was spoken in a light, even joking, manner. She needed to get closer to him and while this should have scared her, discovering the truth pushed her forward. "I'm sorry that we had to leave so quickly yesterday. We never got to know much about you."

Casey reached for a control that dangled down from a wire. "Not really much to know and now's not the time. We've got work to do. Stand back."

She did as he said. She wasn't going to test out how she'd fare against the ribbons.

As the beans tossed, Casey pushed something else

and a pressurized spray coated the beans. It was just as Jimmy had described the process earlier that day.

Casey let go of the controller and waved for her to follow him out of the room. "That will mix for twenty-five minutes. It's set on a timer to stop. Now we go on to the next room."

"I do have a question. Where does the spray come from? I mean it's obvious we're adding the flavor to the beans by that method. Who is responsible for making the flavoring?"

"It's all measured out in the company's lab. There is a science to all of this, you know. It's not as easy as grabbing a cup of coffee and enjoying it. Not once you see what goes on behind the scenes."

She found Casey's tone even more defensive than his words, and it did nothing to weaken her suspicions about him. If anything, it served to strengthen them. He had moved across the country, taken a pay cut, received miscellaneous deposits in his bank account, and now, as it turned out, was obsessed with the coffee process.

Chapter 32

And the Key Fits

Sean wasn't sure what he was supposed to accomplish as a janitor, besides giving himself a stomach ache and learning how to bring up the shine in a dull floor. But as he mopped he realized the one thing in his favor was the time to think.

First of all, Dee Dee had said that cyanide wasn't easy to come by. She did mention it was in natural substances such as apples. It was another thing that made Casey seem even more capable of being a corporate spy and saboteur. But as Sean worked his way through the numerous corridors, he came across a room that had a sign next to it that read *Quality Control.* He tried the handle and it was locked. Letting go of the mop altogether and leaning it against the wall, he pulled out a ring full of keys that the not-so-sweet HR lady had given him. He still didn't have her name. It wasn't something she had been forthcoming with.

Thumbing through all the keys, he wondered why they hadn't upgraded to keycards. It would have made everything so much easier. He found one labeled QC and shoved it into the lock. It released, and he twisted the handle.

"Excuse me! You can't go in there. What do you think you're doing?" The human resources lady was huffing it toward him, her arms moving wildly at her sides.

Sean let go of the handle. "I was going to clean in

there. It is an office?"

"No. You don't have clearance to clean in there. This is your first night."

Sean didn't verbalize the thought he had. If the company was concerned about restricting certain areas maybe he shouldn't have a key for it. Also, with her emphasis on this being his first shift, no one seemed to care that he was running around on his own.

"I don't clean in there?"

"Not yet you don't. Give me that key."

Sean handed over the ring and met with a gruff exhale as she swiped it from him and worked to free the key.

He thought he'd press his already unfortunate luck. "Why don't I clean in there?"

"Because this is where the beans are given a final taste before they are approved for the consumer. It's also where all the flavor recipes are kept. We can't have new hires getting in there and possibly messing things up."

Sean assessed her and realized how worked up she was getting over this. "I didn't mean to upset you."

"Don't flatter yourself. It takes a lot to upset me. This wasn't quite enough." She dropped the key ring into his open palm.

He was curious, though. If this wasn't upset, what was?

"All right, well, keep on. Don't let me stop you from mopping the rest of the place." She gestured up and down the hallway and then took off in one direction.

Sean squeezed the mop head in the bucket and watched after her. Casey Park seemed to have motive for poisoning the beans, but Sean had to wonder why the HR lady appeared so unhappy with her employment.

On top of that, why the quality control department was kept under such tight wraps. Was it just to protect the recipes from the competition or something more?

Chapter 33

Logistics

Jimmy heard the beeping of a forklift backing up. When he turned to see where it was coming from, it performed a tight spin and headed straight for him. He didn't think it was slowing down either.

"Watch out," Jimmy cried out, even though it shouldn't have been necessary. The forks were empty and the driver would have a clear line of sight.

Jimmy stepped out of the way, but the driver torqued the wheel at the last minute to change course and miss him. The machine stopped and the man jumped down. He might have even left his seat before the thing came to a complete stop.

"Who are you?"

"I'm Gavin. This is my first day. Are you Luke?"

"I am."

As soon as he got within sniffing range, Jimmy's eyes watered. He wondered when Luke might have showered last and guessed it was probably days ago unless he had a medical condition that had him sweating excessively.

Luke snatched the clipboard Jimmy held. "Now, you and I will be local late afternoon deliveries and then loading up the trucks for the next day. We also prepare waybills for Hasty Parcel Service. That will start around eight o'clock."

Jimmy stifled his amusement over the fact that Tasty used Hasty. Where did people come up with their business names?

"We don't deliver all the coffee?"

His question met with derisive laughter. "We only do deliveries within a two-hour driving radius of the plant. Otherwise, we hire Hasty to deliver the coffee."

"So, for out of state customers, such as those in New York State?"

"Yes, since that would be outside of the two-hour driving radius, wouldn't it."

"You're right."

"Uh-huh." Luke stopped all movement and stared at Jimmy. "Where are you from anyway?"

"The agency."

He waved a hand. "No, I mean you didn't grow up in Virginia, did you?"

"New York State."

"I thought so. I could tell by the accent."

Jimmy didn't know how to respond. It was strange being confronted with the thought that he had an accent.

"And speaking of the agency, you're only going to be here a brief time. They did tell you that?"

"Yes." This was the second time it was emphasized to him that this job was temporary.

"You're just here because we've got a heavy load right now and you're to help with the possible transition."

"The transition?"

"Yeah. Oh, man, they didn't tell you, did they?" Luke shook his head. "We might not have any drivers soon."

"What do you mean?"

"Everything is probably getting moved over to Hasty. It has something to do with the company's costs involved with running its own trucks and full-time drivers. If you ask me, they take the trucks and drivers away, there goes our personal touch."

"Personal touch?"

"Yeah, we're the only coffee company who offers such a service. Our biggest competitor, Java Worldwide, only delivers via hired couriers, even in their own city."

Jimmy nodded as his mind ruminated on what he was being told. Everywhere he seemed to turn at Tasty Beans, despite the cheery shirts, no one was happy. Most wore scowls and responded with clipped remarks. There was more going on inside this company than poison. And that was saying a lot.

Chapter 34

Coffee and Chitchat

Sara sent Jimmy to pick up coffee from Dunkin' Donuts. As for food, they had that at the hotel as it seemed like a waste not to take part in the breakfast buffet when likely so much food was thrown out already. She just wanted to make sure her hot, steaming beverage wasn't poisoned, and the chain was the best way to go. Even still, she used the test strips on everyone's coffee. They all came back clear.

Sean was smiling at her as she took her first sip, but he didn't say anything. Based on the implication that he thought she was being paranoid, she glanced at Jimmy and then back to Sean. "How did the toilet scrubbing go, darling?"

"So wonderful that I think I'm going to quit."

She laughed. "You've never been a quitter."

"I don't know about that," Jimmy chimed in.

"Leaving my job as a cop doesn't count. Besides, I'm technically still doing the job, just without all the red tape."

"And using a mop." Jimmy chuckled and Sean balled up a napkin and threw it across the room. Jimmy caught it. "Sorry, I couldn't help it."

"Uh-huh." Sean took a draw on his coffee. "You go first, Sara. Tell us about Casey."

"As you know, we're still waiting for Adam to get back to us on the money transfers. Hopefully, we find out something more there before we go in today." Sean had told her he tried Adam on his break last night.

"Do you think you're in danger?"

It was a question Sean had asked her more times than she could count and she had a superb memory. She appreciated his concern, even understood it, but she wondered when he would realize his worrying about her was unnecessary. She could take care of herself, but she didn't want to get involved with that topic of conversation in front of Jimmy right now.

"I'm safe, Sean." She wondered if her response was premature. Some of the machines at Tasty Beans would be capable of inflicting great harm, potentially even death. She'd leave the ribbon blender out of the discussion. "Casey seemed very defensive when it came to the flavoring aspect of the business. He said that the formula is determined and prepared by the lab."

"So no one else has access to modify them?" Sean asked.

"I'm not sure yet. Casey is very conservative. He only says what he needs to and nothing more."

"That's what one would expect of a corporate spy and potential murderer," Jimmy added.

Sara let her gaze wander to him. His hand dangled past the length of the chair arm and the way he swayed the cup he held, it appeared empty.

"What about you, Jimmy?"

"Everyone in the shipping department is miserable. The man who is training me is named Luke. He stinks like you wouldn't believe. If we were around next Christmas, I'd buy him a bar of soap. Scratch that, I might gift it now just because."

"You said everyone was miserable?" Sean prompted.

Sara's eyes went to her husband. She loved the man

for what he was sacrificing for this case. She loved the fact that, despite his periodic complaining, he followed through on taking care of his undercover job.

"Oh yeah. Both the manager, a man named Bruce, and Luke emphasized that my job is temporary."

Sara leaned forward, resting her elbows on her knees. "Did they say why?"

"Apparently Tasty Beans is considering Hasty Parcel Service for all their del—"

"Wait a minute, Tasty hires Hasty." Sean turned to her with a smirk on his face.

Jimmy hitched his shoulders. "I thought the same thing when I first heard, but hey, I didn't name the businesses."

"Go ahead."

"Anyway, as I was saying, rumor has it that the drivers may lose their jobs to the courier company."

Sara sat back. "That could be motive. Poison the beans and take the company down with you."

"But over a rumor?" Sean stressed.

"They are pretty sure of it, Sean. They might be rumors, but the people in the shipping department are taking them as gospel." Jimmy set the cup on the table next to him.

"And how would someone in the shipping department poison the beans when they're already packaged and sealed by the time…" Sean stopped talking. "That's one area we overlooked. I know we have to clear Casey first, but no one is beyond suspicion."

"That's right," Sara agreed.

"What's to say that the cyanide isn't being added at the point of packaging?"

Sara studied both men and replied. "Nothing, I suppose. As I said, Casey seemed pretty adamant that the flavoring aspect is not to be questioned."

"Does he have access to the packaging department?"

"That's the next step from flavoring."

"What about quality control?" Sean asked.

"Quality control? What about it? Although it would make sense."

"When I was cleaning yesterday I came across a door labeled as that department."

"It's not even something that Adam mentioned," Jimmy said.

"That's strange, he's normally so thorough," Sara added.

"When we left Albany our sole focus was on Casey. He's assigned to the flavoring department. The human resources lady mentioned they check the coffee as the last step, but it's possible that quality checks are conducted at different points along the process."

"So you're thinking maybe Casey has access to the coffee after that and is adding the cyanide then—somewhere between quality control and shipping?" Sara summarized.

"That's exactly what I'm thinking."

Chapter 35

Put Through the Wringer

Sean dialed Adam on his cell phone. When he answered, Sean announced, "You're on speaker. The three of us are here."

"Hi, everyone."

Jimmy and Sara spoke at the same time to greet Adam.

Sean preferred to ignore the deflated tone in Adam's voice. "We're after an update on Casey."

"I was afraid of that when I saw your name on caller ID."

"No success so far?"

"Not much anyhow. Whoever is responsible for that money going into Casey's account each month is hard to pin down."

Sean caught something in the way Adam worded his reply. "You tracked it down to some point, didn't you?"

"There's nothing that eludes you is there?"

"Except for our killer right now, and the longer we take to put everything together the more people might die."

"I am working as fast as I can."

Sean noticed the defensiveness in Adam's voice. At the same time, Sara placed her hand on the back of Sean's. It was her gentle reminder to take it easy on him.

"We know you are, Adam," Sara reassured him. "You do have something, though, don't you?"

"I do and I don't. The money traced back to a law office in Austin, Texas. Trying to find out why they are sending Casey money, that is harder to figure out."

Sara tugged Sean's arm for his attention. "It could be that Java Worldwide is routing the payments through the law office to cover their tracks."

"I thought of the same thing, Sara. Just before you called I had started researching firms that Java Worldwide work with, and they don't have any connection to this particular one."

"It doesn't mean that Java isn't behind this," Sara said.

"No, it doesn't. They might be using it because it's not one of their regular ones." Adam paused a few seconds. "So, as you can see, I am making some progress, but not getting far. Maybe I can hack into the firm's records and figure it out that way."

"Just keep on it." Sean realized it probably wasn't necessary to verbalize the request in so many words, but the enormity of this case kept hitting him in waves. There really wasn't any time to waste.

"Will do."

Sean hung up and turned to Jimmy and Sara. "Thoughts?"

Sara spoke first. "I still think that Casey is involved. Everything we know about him is suspicious. A move across the country for a pay cut. Money from a mysterious law office."

"I'm with Sara," Jimmy said.

"See if you can confirm Casey's access to shipping and quality control."

"I will, Sean."

"I'm going to see if I can get into that office." Sean turned to Jimmy. "How did your deliveries go yesterday, by the way? Did you meet any customers?"

"I did, and none of them seemed to be ill, but I noticed the labels on the boxes. Surprising that for their trademark flavor, none that I delivered were dark cherry almond."

"There's a connection to that specific flavor."

"Sean, we know it's their signature flavor. That could be enough right there."

Chapter 36

Beans for Two

Sara let herself into the flavoring area and tucked her wig into the white cap. The first time she'd put it on she had worried about it coming off her head, along with the fake locks, but today she was confident everything would stay in place.

Casey came through the swinging door. "What are you doing in here?"

"What do you mean? I thought this is where I'm supposed to be."

"You always wait for me."

His statement sparked something else. Yesterday they had passed other flavoring rooms. Each of them had a panel of windows so that people could see inside. Maybe it was another quality control process? Sara wasn't sure, but she remembered that there were teams of two in each room. No one worked alone. It must have something to do with preventing tampering, or maybe safety around those large blenders? But if she was Casey's partner, then how long had he worked by himself?

He kept his eyes on her as he put his cap in place.

"I apologize for getting ahead of myself."

"Just don't let it happen again."

"I was hoping you'd be able to take me on a bit of a tour."

"On a tour? No way, we don't have time for something

like that."

"I know we didn't do this yesterday, but do we ever get involved with quality control or packaging?" She didn't like the way his eyes glazed over when she asked the question. Was he on to her? It was time to put on the girlie innocence routine. "I just figured that someone must taste the coffee to make sure the blends come out the way they should. You know, for company reputation and all."

"We do have people who do that all along the way."

"Do we?"

"We do."

Sara's heart thumped. "We do? As in us specifically?"

"Yes. I just did it after you left shift yesterday. We were moving slower so I put in some overtime."

Apparently training a new hire was a real inconvenience.

"You did which exactly—taste testing or something to do with packaging?" She just wanted to be certain.

"Taste testing. Then it goes to packaging."

"I assume we'll sample the product together on this shift?" She swallowed roughly, the thought of cyanide rolling in her mind, but she realized the stupidity of that. Casey wouldn't poison the coffee before tasting it. When they drank it, it would be perfectly safe—assuming Casey was the one behind the poisoning. Was she willing to take the risk that a small dose wouldn't hurt her?

"If we get on with things, there's that possibility." He huffed past her and went into the first room and stopped short of the controller. "You go ahead and I'll watch you today. You do remember what I taught you yesterday?"

"Yes." She went over to the controller that dangled

from the wire and held it in her hand. “I noticed that everyone works in pairs. Why is that?”

“You just push the green button to start the ribbons turning.”

“Before me, who worked with you?”

“Listen, if you want to talk all shift, I’ll have to go to HR.”

Whoa. This guy really didn’t like conversation, and he particularly didn’t care for it when it revolved around Tasty Beans and procedure. For a man in the position of training a new employee, it didn’t sit well with Sara.

Chapter 37

Aftertaste

Sean was determined to get into the quality control office with or without the key, but he had to wait until the employees from that part of the building went home. After quick assessment it seemed that time had finally come.

Before leaving Sara, he had gotten one of her bobby pins. Armed with nothing more than this to get him inside, he hoped it was enough to pick the lock. To think, yesterday he was cursing the dated hardware and today it could be what made everything easier. He preferred the old locks over the modern keycard contraptions. Where he was out of luck was with a cover story. He couldn't come up with one for the life of him and hoped that, if faced with the need to conjure one, it would miraculously come to him.

After another scan down the hallway—in both directions—Sean slipped the pin in and got to work. Seconds later, he turned the handle and stepped inside.

He took his mop and bucket with him, deciding that if anyone was in there, he'd say he was cleaning. If he ran into someone who was aware of the cleaning schedule, he'd use the excuse of being a new person. Hopefully, that would be all it took.

The door opened to a hallway. Lit fluorescents hummed above and went the length of the corridor. Three offices branched off on the right. Two of them were dark and locked. The last one was open and light streamed into the hall.

Sean took out his mop and whistled a tune.

"Who is there?" It was a female voice.

"Just cleaning, ma'am." He thought the latter was a nice touch. He kept washing the floor or sopping it anyway. He could handle never smelling mop water for the rest of his life.

"What are you—" The woman braced herself against the doorframe, almost panting for breath.

He didn't have Sara's precise memory, but he swore that was a sign of cyanide poisoning.

He stopped cleaning. "Are you all right?"

"I'm fine, but you shouldn't be here right now." She coughed. "I have work to do."

Sean noticed how she was getting more winded with every word. Either she excited easily, like pretty much everyone else at Tasty Beans or something was wrong here.

"Oh." She swayed left. Then right.

Sean let go of the mop and the handle banged against the floor. He steadied her balance and assessed her office. It was a nice size, but its potential was masked by clutter. "You should sit down." He helped her to her chair and searched desperately for a nameplate, but there wasn't one. He spotted a half-empty coffee cup. "What is your name?"

"Susan. I don't feel so—" She vomited and barely missed Sean.

That was all it took. Blown cover or not, this woman was going to die if he didn't get her help. He pulled out his cell phone and dialed 9-1-1.

Chapter 38

Feigning Illness

With the bay doors open, Jimmy heard the approaching sirens. It was definitely an ambulance, and, from the sounds of it, turning into the lot for Tasty Beans.

He stopped keying information into the computer. The waybill could wait. "Someone must be hurt." He said this to Luke, who sat beside him and watched his every move. The man wasn't a good teacher, but he had observation down pat, and he had no problem pointing out what was being done incorrectly.

"Keep pecking away. It's just an ambulance."

The man's reaction made Jimmy wonder something. "Do they come here a lot?"

"Just keep—" Luke waved his arm toward the computer.

The motion fanned a breeze of underarm odor right up Jimmy's nose. It hit just right. He managed to grab a tissue from a nearby box just before he sneezed. "Sorry 'bout that." Jimmy found it ironic how he was making the apology when it was Luke's lack of hygiene that caused it to let rip in the first place.

"Don't mention it."

Jimmy thought he'd try asking the question again. "Do ambulances come here a lot?"

"Are you asking if we have a poor safety record? Then the answer is no. If you're simply asking if an ambulance has been here before, then the answer is yes."

It was more than this guy's odor that was giving him a headache. Talk about speaking in riddles.

"Why did it come the last time?" Jimmy pecked a few keys and completed the waybill for one shipment. He picked up the paperwork for the next and started on it.

"Someone in the quality control department wasn't feeling well."

"What was it?"

"It just turned out to be some sort of bug."

"Seems extreme to get an ambulance for the flu."

"Yeah, tell me about it. Ever since this happened about a month ago, she's been pegged with a nickname. Pandemonium Sue. She'll never live it down."

"So she's fine now?"

"I said it was a virus. She was fine within the week."

Jimmy turned his attention to the waybills and, from what his supervisor would see, he was working. But while his hands moved to do the job, his mind was on Pandemonium Sue. Then it went to Sean and Sara. What if the ambulance was for one of them?

He stood to leave.

"Hey, where are you going?"

"I'm not feeling so hot myself. I've got to use the can." That's what he told Luke.

Chapter 39

Fine Grind

Sara was going through the motions as Casey directed while being careful not to let him get too close. She especially didn't want him coming up on her from behind. All he'd need to do was push her into one of those blenders if he felt she was getting too nosey. She wasn't going to take a chance on the man being partial to one murder method. All he'd have to say is that he tripped and it was all an accident.

As she watched the ribbons rotate, her mind conducted a similar process. It blended what she knew so far. Casey had confirmed access to testing the flavors before they'd go to packaging. Being the last stop before that happened, it would be relatively easy for Casey to poison the beans at that point, especially if he were working solo. She wondered how long he had been.

The alarm buzzed, notifying the plant employees that it was time for the dinner break. The timing was ideal for her and Casey as they had just added flavoring to a batch and it needed to turn for twenty-five minutes.

Casey opened the door for her. Once she was past him, she realized she had briefly let her guard down and had let him get behind her. She spun to face him and walked backward. "Eat with me?"

"I guess. What would your hubby think about that?"

"It's just dinner. Besides he doesn't have to know." She smiled at him and met with a grin. Casey was a man after all. He must simply be leery of new people and, based on what he may have done, with good reason.

"So who worked with you before me?" she asked, hoping that since they were on their own time now and not the company's he might be more straightforward.

"He left."

"Oh, simple as that? Did he get another job?"

"I'm not sure."

"How long were you on your own?"

"What is this, twenty questions? If you're going to have dinner with me, I'd rather talk about you." His arm no sooner touched her shoulder than it dropped.

Sean was hurrying straight for them, his face a wash of panic. She almost blurted out his real name. "What is it?"

He put his hands on her arms, bracing her from the front. "Susan in the quality control department was—" Sean glanced at Casey.

"Was what?" she prompted.

"She's not feeling well. Can we talk?"

"Sure. Excuse me, Casey."

Sean took her to a quiet corner of the lunchroom. "She was poisoned."

"Are you sure?"

"Her symptoms were just like Beverly Sparks'. I was there."

"You were there?"

"I'm the one that called the ambulance."

"Oh my word, Sean." She touched his cheek. "Are you okay?"

"I'm fine. Let's go." He took her hand and led her out the front of the building.

Other employees were gathered around where the ambulance was parked, and two paramedics were loading a lady into it. Jimmy was standing at the edge of the crowd, moving this way and that, obviously trying to get a line of sight.

"Jim—Gavin," Sara called out to him.

She and Sean jogged toward him.

"Thank heavens you two are okay. I was worried sick but thought this would be the best place to come to know for sure. Do you know what happened? Rumor is flying all over that it was Pandemonium Sue up to her old tricks."

"There seems to be a lot of flying rumors." Sean moved in closer to Jimmy. "And what do you mean by her old tricks?"

"Apparently she was taken away in an ambulance before, for a stomach bug, but within the week she was back to work."

"When was this?"

"A month ago, according to Luke."

Sean signaled for them to move farther off to the side.

Once there, Sara said, "So she was sick a month ago and now she is again? That's too much of a coincidence."

"Not to mention that I was there with her. She was dizzy and almost lost her balance. She was sick on the floor. Oh, and she was out of breath."

"All symptoms of cyanide poisoning, Sean. The doctors were wrong to assume she had a bug last time."

"Possibly dead wrong."

Chapter 40

An Unforgettable Woman

Sara had noticed that while most people had gathered in clusters, one woman stood alone, her arms crossed. She had black tresses and a pale complexion.

The woman must have sensed Sara's observation of her and had turned to face her, holding the gaze for a few seconds before going inside the building.

Sara wasn't sure whether this interaction had meant anything, but she recalled it later that night when the three of them were brainstorming in her and Sean's hotel room.

"I can't believe I was right there and couldn't help her." Sean sipped on a cognac while Jimmy drank a Scotch, and Sara stuck with water.

The word had come back before the end of shift that Susan Gallacher had died on the way to the hospital.

"Guess she caused pandemonium for a reason. She did have something to worry about," Jimmy mumbled before placing his empty glass on the table next to him.

"We need to call Adam and let him know the latest news."

"Let me do that, Sean." She dialed Adam on speaker and he answered on the first ring.

"I was just going to call you. I've been at this all day and I've finally got some things sorted out."

"Adam, we need to tell you something first."

"What is it, Sara?"

"Another woman is dead. Poisoned."

"I agree that we have to get the person responsible for this, but I don't think it's Casey Park," Adam said.

Sean audibly gulped down his mouthful of cognac. "What about the money and the move? How can all of that be explained?"

"The law firm that made the deposits to his account specializes in estates."

"It was an inheritance," Sara stated.

"Yes. His great aunt died and left him everything. She was worth a fair amount and chose to have it divvied out to him."

"It's just coincidental that it was around the same time that he took a pay cut and moved across the country?"

"There's a good reason for that too. Casey Park's aunt died in November. Part of the stipulation for him to get the money was that he move to Williamsburg."

"Why, I wonder."

"So did I. So I did more digging. Casey's cousin lives in town."

"His great aunt's child?"

"That's right, living in a long-term care facility for people with mental issues. Another part of the deal was that Casey was to visit his cousin periodically."

"Terrific work, Adam, except for one thing. It leaves us without a suspect." Sean swirled his glass, the ice cubes clinking against the sides.

"Not exactly." Sara filled the men in on the woman who had been standing alone. "She was in formal attire, the kind that would be required of office personnel, possibly even management."

"It could explain why she was there when most of the office staff had already left for the day," Sean added.

"Adam, check out the employee records for a woman in her twenties who works in the office."

"Will do, Sara."

"Call us back the second you have anything. I don't care when it is."

Sara ended the call. "We were so certain it was Casey we didn't truly open our eyes to other possibilities. He seemed to have everything lined up in his favor, or against him, depending on how you look at it. But think about this, whoever is poisoning the coffee beans probably has access to all levels of processing."

"Hopefully, that will narrow it down some," Sean said.

Chapter 41

The Latest Findings

Sean's ringing phone woke them up. "Hello."

"It's Adam."

"Just a sec." Sean put him on speaker so Sara could hear.

"I've got a few women who match the criteria you mentioned last night. I forwarded them to your phone just before I called you."

"Hang on." Sean brought up the message and held the pictures out so that Sara could see them.

"That's her. Number three."

"Number three is Melissa Oliver. She works in the accounting department. She's mid-level so I'm not exactly sure why she would have been there so late. Maybe they were behind and she was helping out. I don't know. But I did some digging. Melissa's background is clean, but she's married to another employee of Tasty Beans."

"Who?"

"Name's Luke Oliver."

"Luke?" Sara sat up. "That's the first name of the man who is training Jimmy. Is he in shipping, Adam?"

"You got it."

"Assuming they are behind the poisoning, we need a motive."

"We also need to know if either of them has access to cyanide."

"Let me solve that riddle for both of you. Melissa's dad works in a lab."

"Dee Dee had mentioned that cyanide's locked up in pharmaceutical labs," Sara said.

Adam continued. "Melissa's dad works in one that would definitely have it around. It is used to measure urine ketone bodies as a follow-up for diabetic patients."

"So Melissa got her hands on the cyanide from her father's lab and poisoned the beans. But why?"

Sara jumped from the bed. "I know why, Sean. Remember Jimmy said that Tasty Beans was going to switch over all their deliveries to a parcel company? That would mean that Luke Oliver would lose his job."

"That sounds like possible motive to me," Adam said.

Sara continued. "Being in accounting, Melissa would have access to all departments. No doubt she'd collect reports from the section heads too."

"We have to figure out if she has a reason for being there so late last night and get some proof on her." Sean realized he was the unwanted voice of reason the moment he spoke and Sara narrowed her eyes, but it was the hard fact of life.

"Proof as in?" Sara asked.

"As in cyanide on her person. Indisputable proof she has access to the flavoring labs. Something. If it had to do with her husband losing his job, why not just poison management?"

"All good questions, Sean. Adam, we'll take it from here."

"Take care."

"You got it."

Sean studied his wife's face. He recognized the hunger there and assumed it likely mirrored his own. They were close to stopping a killer and had to watch every move to make sure she was held responsible. “There is one major issue I just thought of. If word gets out that Susan died of cyanide poisoning, it might scare off Melissa.”

“She’ll likely go into hiding, or stop the poisoning for a while.”

“When you saw her, did you think she seemed upset?”

“I’d say upset, but not sad.”

“So we could be dealing with a psychotic.”

“Jimmy and I are anyhow. Didn’t you get fired?”

“Not yet, but I’m sure I will be today.”

Chapter 42

Called Out

If this was the last time Jimmy saw this place, he'd be all too happy. Not that he was opposed to manual labor, or even spending time glued to a desk, but to be placed in such an environment as Tasty Beans was its own version of cruel and unusual punishment. No one wanted to be there, as evidenced by their attitudes. And now, after receiving the update on Adam's findings and the McKinleys' hunches, he was working tightly with the suspect's husband.

Everything had taken on a heightened sense of urgency since Susan had lost her life the night before. The gossip firing around carried no mention of the woman's nickname, but it did include talk about poison.

So far it seemed the media had kept the exact type out of the limelight, but Jimmy figured it would only be a matter of time before the words *death by cyanide* were plastered across page one.

Even without reporters, the damage was done. Tasty Beans employees were talking about customer complaints and a few had left their shifts early claiming to feel weak. The local hospitals would be overloaded by them claiming illness—real or imagined—and the medical profession would have Melissa to thank.

Luke came up behind Jimmy—he hadn't heard his steps, but that was definitely his smell.

"Good afternoon," Jimmy said.

"Yeah, it is."

Jimmy needed mind-reading abilities because it was hard to tell if Luke was upset about Susan's death or something else. Either way, it was apparent his mood was riper than usual. This guy made talking to Albert Needham seem like a walk in the park.

Luke grabbed the clipboard off the wall. "You're driving today."

Jimmy felt around in his pockets. "Ah, shoot."

"You forgot your license again?"

"What can I say?"

"You're incompetent for one." He hooked the clipboard back in place and studied Jimmy.

"You said the agency sent you."

"Yes, I did."

"Interesting, because I called them after you left me hanging to go ambulance watching."

The wad of saliva was thick going down Jimmy's throat.

"I called to give them what for, for sending someone like you to me. You know what they said? They said, and I paraphrase here. 'We have his name in our records, but no one remembers screening him. We apologize for this oversight.' I thought that was pretty interesting. How does someone slip through? That has never happened with this agency before."

"The girl who interviewed me really wasn't feeling well that day."

"It seems there's a lot of that going on."

"She was really tired like she had a hard night. She probably just forgot."

Seconds passed and Jimmy wasn't sure if Luke was going to accept his explanation. As a cop, Jimmy would have busted Luke for such an obvious tale.

Luke took the clipboard in his hands again. "Guess I'll drive. Actually, I've got to run some signed packing slips up to accounting first."

"Hey, let me do it. You know, to make up for the license thing."

"Sure."

Chapter 43

A Man's Gotta Do...

Sean waited outside human resources. The receptionist sent him back with a security escort. It was the same guy from two days ago.

"I've got it from here. Thanks." Sean waved at him, hoping he'd leave, but no such luck. He took a seat a few chairs down. Sean was definitely getting fired.

"Stephan," the woman bellowed from behind her closed door.

The lady at the front desk must have called and told her he was there.

Sean cracked the door, hoping that he'd be fired while at the same time, wishing for the opposite. If he was still employed, maybe he could work his way up to accounting and meet Melissa Oliver in person, or snoop around in her office.

"Sit." After he had followed her direction, she continued. "As it turns out, you were somewhere I specifically told you not to go. Is that correct?"

"It is, but it's a good thing I—"

"I don't want to hear about it." The woman sat back and clasped her hands on her expansive stomach. "At the end of the day what matters most is that you disobeyed a direct order. What I want to know is how you got into that room in the first place."

Silence, except for the ticking of a battery-operated clock that more or less *tunked* rather than ticked.

He glanced up at it and watched the second hand go around halfway.

"Mr. Levine, answer me."

"You're right. I shouldn't have been in that room."

"That's not what I asked. I asked how. I took your key."

If he came clean about picking the lock, he'd certainly be fired. He only saw one way to play this and that was honesty. He stood up and made sure the door to the office was locked.

"What are you do—"

He took off the wig.

"Who? What?"

"My real name is Sean McKinley."

"I don't care who you—" Her eyes absorbed his tacky wardrobe, which was another pair of tight-fitted pants, jeans this time, but with no bell-bottoms. As her gaze traveled upward and met his, she said, "You're that man in the news, the one who inherited all that money a while back."

"That's me."

"Where's Sara? Oh, is that Gwen?"

"Yes, it is. Listen, we're investigating something going on within Tasty Beans." He wanted to bring up that they were licensed PIs but being issued from New York State would mean nothing here.

"Let me guess, it has to do with the poisoning?"

Her directness had Sean's hand going to the doorknob.

"Don't be nervous." She must have noticed his reaction. "Sit. I can't tell you how excited I am to meet you." She fluttered her hand next to her chest and then extended it to him.

He shook it, despite getting the distinct feeling the woman would have preferred he kissed the back of it.

That. Was. Not. Happening.

"So, this case?" She shifted in the chair and it creaked beneath her. "Ratty ol' thing. I don't even think I introduced myself. It's Wanda."

"Nice to meet you, Wanda." He liked to repeat people's names after an introduction. It was believed that it aided memory.

"You flatter me. Wow, my girlfriends are not going to believe this."

"I need your help. I need to keep my job and my cover intact. We're very close to apprehending the killer."

"I was going to fire you."

"I had a feeling." He held eye contact with her. "Please help me."

"Who do you think it is?"

"I'd rather not say until I know for sure, but I need full reign today, which means I'll require keys for all the departments."

She pointed in the direction of the hall. "Larry was going to escort you from the building." She pressed a few buttons on her phone. "Larry, head back to the front. We've worked things out in here."

"Thank you. You won't regret this." Sean jumped up, put his wig back in place, and gave Wanda one more glance before leaving. He hoped he wouldn't regret disclosing his true identity.

Chapter 44

Scheming

On her third shift, Sara was less concerned about getting caught up in a blender and more concerned about how to stop Melissa Oliver. Two people were already dead and who knew how many more were sick. She'd heard what people were saying. The word poison was being thrown around a lot, although she never heard cyanide, specifically, come up.

Sara wondered if her time might be better used in some other way, seeing as the top suspect was Melissa Oliver. As she watched the spray cover the beans, she realized again that she could be an accomplice of sorts. They had to stop the shipments she'd had a hand in blending no later than tomorrow.

She then thought of Sean and how he was probably getting fired at this exact point in time. It was unfortunate because he was their best shot at gaining entrance to all the departments. Then she realized that every section would report to accounting. Surely there was something that needed to be delivered up there before break. If so, she'd be able to talk to Melissa Oliver and get a feel for her. While the circumstantial evidence seemed damning, it had for Casey too, and that had led to a dead end.

Sean ducked out of Wanda's office, his steps lighter. There was something burdensome about being undercover and hiding one's identity. By stripping away one's name and appearance, everything felt like a lie.

He watched the suds fill the bucket, and when the water reached halfway, he turned off the hose. Accounting was located on the third floor, in the north corner of the building, but he couldn't head up there right away. It was about three thirty. He'd wait it out until after the dinner break. Then he'd let himself into Melissa's office and snoop around. Hopefully, he'd get lucky.

Jimmy rapped on the doorframe to get the younger woman's attention. She was rummaging in the hutch over her desk. She closed it when she heard him.

"Who are you?"

"A new guy in shipping."

"Right. Luke mentioned you. He's my husband. Not sure if he mentioned it to you." She winked at Jimmy.

Just as Sara had described the woman, she was beautiful in a striking *Snow White* sort of way. She was also young. Remorse for her decisions stabbed Jimmy. She had ruined her entire future for—what?—a job. Craziness.

"Please take a seat."

The chair she pointed to was positioned against the wall, not opposite her desk. It was stacked with papers.

"Let me get that." She scooped them into her arms and dropped into her chair again. "Not enough hours in the day, I tell you. Have they got you busy?"

"Yeah, so far." Jimmy noticed that Melissa Oliver was the nicest person he'd met here. She really must be insane. She poisoned without thought to consequence—or maybe she gave it deep consideration—and put on a sincere front. She was the type of killer no one wanted to cross.

She deposited the stack of papers on the floor beside her.

Jimmy had almost forgotten about the paperwork in his own hands. He stretched to reach her without getting up and handed it over to her. "Here you go. I'm guessing it's the day's packing slips for billing."

"Thanks."

"Don't mention it. You must work a lot of overtime with all that." Jimmy bobbed his head toward her desk. He made a quick assessment of her office that would help the three of them later on when they came up to confront Melissa. Her desk was L-shaped, with a hutch, and located in the back left corner of the room. Behind it was a large window. In front was a credenza, and probably the reason the chair for guests needed to be situated just inside the door.

"I'm here pretty much every night until eight o'clock. Sometimes it feels like I'm the only hard worker left. Tonight, I'm out of here at five o'clock. Going to meet up with my dad for a dinner out."

Jimmy pushed the fact that her father was her drug dealer out of his mind. "That's awful about that woman in quality control. What was her name again?" Jimmy played stupid.

"Susan Gallacher. She was a nice lady."

"You knew her well?"

"Not really well. We had lunch a couple times."

Jimmy thought maybe Melissa would offer some sentiments about how sad it all was, but she didn't even bother.

"You better get back to Luke before he blows his top. He's got a temper."

"That's probably a good idea."

Jimmy left, pondering where he'd hide the cyanide in the office if it were him. He didn't see any safes in the room, which he found odd, with her being in the accounting department, but maybe someone else handled the money. It was also possible there was one in that hutch or credenza. In a couple more hours, they'd find out.

Chapter 45

The Best Approach

The alarm sounded for the dinner break. What Casey didn't know was that Sara had no intention of returning to her shift afterward. She let him go his way while she went hers, which was straight out the front door. She met up with Sean and Jimmy on the northeast side of the building.

"Luke's suspicious. He knows I'm not from the agency anyway."

"How did he find that out?" Sean asked.

"Adam missed the fact that a commercial driver's license might come in useful."

"But you shouldn't need one for the size of trucks they use."

"That might be the case, but they still want you to. I did find out the layout of Melissa's office though."

Sara listened to him share his findings and realized something. "We can't all go up to her office. Someone needs to stay with Luke and keep an eye on him. If he gets suspicious, he could make a run for it."

She and Sean looked at Jimmy.

"Let me guess, I'm the lucky winner."

"That you are."

"I think there may be a safe in her hutch or credenza, but I don't know for sure."

"We need to call in the police, Sean."

"Let's get our evidence first."

She consented with a nod, even though she sometimes wondered where she conjured the patience to wait things out. When they confronted Melissa, they could speed things along with the persuasive power of a raised gun, but she preferred not to have to go that far. The fact that they were both armed—and technically licensed—wasn't the point.

The buzzer sounded the end of the break.

"Guess it's back to the grind," Jimmy said.

"Be safe," Sean said.

"Yep. No one dies today."

JIMMY HEADED BACK TO THE shipping area, but he wasn't sure how he was supposed to focus on the job when he was working next to the killer's husband. Surely the man had to know what his wife had done. She had mentioned he had a temper. Maybe he put her up to this or threatened her welfare. One sad thing about society was, there were some men who were not opposed to striking a woman. And in each of those cases, the inability to control their tempers was at the top of the list.

Chapter 46

Snooping for Proof

Sean and Sara went back inside the building, but he didn't pick up his mop and Sara never put on a cap. They weren't worried about protecting their cover stories anymore.

They loaded onto the elevator and Sean pushed the button for the third floor.

"My heart is pounding, Sean. We're so close to stopping her. You know, if we didn't get things wrapped up by tomorrow I'd be stopping the shipments of those poisoned beans one way or another."

"We don't know for sure your batches were poisoned."

"I wouldn't want to risk it."

"I know, darling, and I would have been right by your side stopping the deliveries myself. You do have your gun?"

"I do, but I don't want to use it."

"I don't think we'll have to, but we need to be prepared."

Sara nodded and something inside of him fractured. He pulled her in for a hug.

"It's going to be all right." He felt foolish offering such a reassurance, for two reasons. One, he didn't know the future, and, two, a couple people had already paid with their lives.

The elevator dinged its arrival and the doors opened.

"This way." Sean led her down the hall to where

Jimmy had told them to go.

The good news was the level seemed vacant—no talking and no clicking on keyboards. It would make their snooping a lot easier. They just needed to find cyanide in Melissa's possession.

"This is the one, Sean. Jimmy said it was the last office on the right."

"The door is open."

"I'm sure you'd just pick the lock, like you did for the quality control department."

He had told her all about it last night.

"Yes, I probably would have." He went behind the desk. "I'll check in her hutch. You check the credenza."

The hutch had four doors. He found a safe behind the last one he opened.

"Nothing down here, Sean."

"That's all right. I just found it."

"You've got a safe?"

"I do."

Sean wheeled Melissa's chair out from behind her desk. Sara put it near the door and stood beside him.

The safe was a small number and he was careful taking it out of the cabinet and placing it on the desk. What he had to do next could be risky but he trusted that if Melissa were hiding liquid cyanide she'd make sure it was sealed tightly. They didn't need poisonous vapors filling the air.

"This is even better than I thought it would be."

"It's an electronic safe, Sean. We need a passcode."

"Actually…" Sean banged the top of it with the flat of his hand and then turned the handle. He did this a couple times and then the safe opened.

"I'm not even going to ask."

"Are you impressed?" He hoped to see pride in her

expression, but it was missing, so he explained the process to her. "In cheaper models, the hit releases the tumblers for a brief second. If it had been a combination lock safe, I would have benefited from a stethoscope. One of which I don't have."

Sara angled her head. "You are full of surprises."

He must have read her facial expression incorrectly. "You are impressed." He let his smirk spread.

"I'm just glad we're using it for this side of the law. Although, sometimes the line between right and wrong gets a little fuzzy."

"Sometimes it does." He pulled on the safe door. "Moment of truth."

"What do you think you're doing in here?"

Melissa Oliver was standing in the doorway of her office.

Chapter 47

Never Saw That Coming

Sara drew her weapon on impulse. Her fast reaction took her back to her days as a cop.

"Whoa." Melissa held up her hands. "Who are you people? What are you doing in my safe?"

"You've been poisoning the coffee beans with cyanide," Sara said.

"I haven't been doing—"

"Sean, show her we know." Sara didn't care for the glaze over his eyes. Her stomach dropped.

He pulled out a wad of bills and some checks.

"I find it hard to see how I could have poisoned anyone with money. Although it does have the ability to corrupt people."

Why was she so calm, given the circumstances?

Melissa stepped into the office.

Sara continued. "Your husband was going to lose his job. You're holed up in here every night working overtime. Speaking of which, I heard you were leaving at five today to have dinner with your father. Were you going to get some more cyanide from him?" Sara wasn't worried about giving up Jimmy's cover at this point.

"You've lost your mind." Melissa dropped onto the chair that had been wheeled near the door. "Why would I poison the coffee?"

Sara had to keep going. The guilty often proclaimed their innocence. Melissa was no different. "As I said, your husband's job, your overtime. They probably didn't appreciate all your hard work, all your sacrifice."

"But you're failing to see that it wouldn't be in my best interests to sabotage this company."

Sean's phone rang and he answered it.

Sara kept her eyes on Melissa but listened to Sean's side of the conversation.

He tucked his phone into a pocket. "She's not who we're after."

Melissa turned on Sara. "I told you."

Sean put his hand on Sara's shoulder. "Melissa has significant stock investments with the company. It diminishes her motive."

Sara felt her stance falter slightly and corrected it. "Why didn't that get pointed out to us before?"

Sean guided her arms down and Melissa let out a deep breath once the gun was lowered. Sara put it away.

"If it's not her, who is it, Sean?"

"It needs to be someone who has access to the flavoring lab."

"That is all done in the quality control department and that leaves about a handful of people." Melissa shrugged. "Hey, I want to be helpful. You thought I was a killer? I don't even like to kill flies. I shoo them away hoping they'll leave me alone."

"Give us some names, Melissa," Sean said.

"Myself, the owner, his wife, his two kids…" Melissa snapped her fingers. "And Wanda from human resources."

Sean's hands went to the desk and he stretched out. "Crap."

"What is it, darling?"

"Darling?" Melissa parroted Sara.

Sara had a feeling why he was reaching for support

to remain upright. "You told her who we are. That's why you're not fired. You didn't mention we were after Melissa, did you?"

"No, don't be crazy."

Sara took a few staggered breaths. "We've got to get her, Sean. That is if she hasn't left for the day."

"I assume you're talking about Wanda? You mentioned getting fired so that would have to be her. Anyway, I just passed her on the way up. She was getting off the elevator when I was getting on."

Sara stared at Sean. "Wanda works on the main level."

"She added more poison to the flavoring mix."

The quality control department was on the fourth floor.

Sean and Sara bounded out from behind the desk and came face to face with Melissa.

"You're going to fix that safe, right? It's Tasty Beans property."

"It's not really broken, but I tell you what, I'll buy a new one. State of the art. One that can't be opened with a well-placed smack and twist of the lever."

Melissa's eyes widened.

Chapter 48

On the Move

Jimmy hated the fact that he was left to babysit Smelly Luke while Sean and Sara got the real killer. Another couple hours of sitting beside the man and making out waybills would be hard time to put in.

"You."

He recognized the voice and swiveled his chair to see Casey Park standing behind him.

"You are a friend of Gwen's."

Jimmy glanced at Luke, then back to Casey. "I am. Why?"

"She didn't show up after dinner. She just left me hanging. Do you have any idea where I can find her? Her husband seems to be missing too."

"I'm sorry, I don't—"

The overweight human resources lady stepped out from behind Casey.

"His name's not Gavin Rossdale. It's Jimmy Voigt."

Jimmy's heart fell to the pit of his stomach, he was sure of it.

Luke jumped to his feet, his finger pointed at Jimmy. "I knew you were a fraud. You're fired!"

"Suits me. I was going to quit anyhow."

"What is going on?" Casey's brow was hitched with confusion.

"Security is going to see the bunch of them out," the woman answered.

"I don't even think Gwen's in the building, is she?" Casey asked.

"She is. You don't seem to appreciate the fact that I have eyes everywhere. I am everywhere."

That's how she had caught Sean trying to get into quality control the first time. She must have been away from the security cameras when Sean returned and picked the lock. As his mind chewed on the fact, the revelation came to him at hurtling speed. The human resources lady was the killer. It was true, he didn't yet know if she had access to cyanide or her motivation. But with her position, it would make sense that she had authorization to enter every department.

The time to keep quiet was past. "It's you." Jimmy stood. "You're the killer."

"What is he talking—Wanda?" This was from Casey.

Wanda, the not-so-sweet human resources lady, could really move for a big woman. Apparently no one should be fooled by a person's size and how that factored in to their agility. She was already at the other end of the shipping dock.

Jimmy tried to keep up, but the last couple mornings of eating a buffet breakfast weren't working in his favor. And if that wasn't enough, his phone was ringing.

"IT'S POSSIBLE WANDA'S STILL IN the building, Sean."

They took the stairs down instead of waiting for the elevator. Sean was on his cell, trying to reach Jimmy. "He's not answering."

"I don't have a good feeling about this."

"Me either."

They reached the lobby and set out into a full run

toward the HR office. The door was locked, but it wouldn't stop Sean from picking it. Sara tossed her wig on the floor.

"Here, take a pin."

"Don't mind if I do."

He worked the lock while Sara called Adam. "Adam, we need a complete background on Wanda—you don't know her last name, Sean?"

He shook his head.

"She works in human resources. I'll hold. Get me everything you can. Criminal background and any potential accessibility to cyanide."

Sean turned the handle. They were in. He pointed to the purse hanging on the coat tree in the corner. "She's still in the building."

"We have to hurry."

"Jimmy can handle himself. I know he can." He rummaged through the desk, searching for a compartment or safe that she might keep the cyanide in.

"So, you are certain he can take care of himself, but still wonder about me sometimes?"

He stopped moving and turned to her. "I love you, Sara."

"I know, and you'd die if anything happened to me."

"I would."

"Trust me that I'd never let anything happen as far as I could control."

"I'm sorry."

She nodded.

He had a weakness when it came to letting go of certain inclinations—jealousy and possession—he didn't really like that last word. He wasn't so much possessive as protective. Yes, that was a better definition.

Still, she was right. He had every reason to trust her. "We're good?"

"Of course, darling." She hustled about the room and stood next to the coat tree. "Melissa said that she ran into Wanda exiting the elevator. She had already delivered the poison. We're likely only going to find an empty bottle or container."

"Unless she dumped it along the way."

"And risk us finding it? No way."

Sara took Wanda's purse off the hook and, in two seconds of rooting through it, came out with an empty bottle, save a drop or three inside.

"Apparently, Wanda didn't think things through. How much do you want to bet this tests positive for cyanide?" Sara asked.

"I'd wager everything I have, but we don't have time to confirm it right now."

"You're right. What should we do with the bottle? Take it with us?"

"I'll hide it and secure it in the janitor closet."

"She'd think of there, wouldn't she?"

"Why would she? We're going to leave her purse right here, and it appears untouched. Besides, she's not going to get the chance to go snooping for it. Let's go see if Jimmy needs our help."

Chapter 49

Improvising

Jimmy wouldn't claim it was his best idea ever, but he had to give himself some credit. He hopped onto the forklift and was happy to find the keys in the ignition. How hard could it be to drive?

He got behind the wheel, and to the right of it were four levers. What each one did, he had no idea. He put it in forward gear, just like one would in a car, and hit the gas.

Luke and Casey were screaming out about not wrecking the machine, but he ignored them. There was a killer to catch.

Wanda was a good distance ahead of him and took the time to turn around to gauge her pursuer's distance. She cried out when she saw the forklift steaming after her. When she faced forward again, she lost her footing, her ankle twisted, and down she went—crumpled like an unmanned marionette—onto an empty pallet.

He slowed his speed and started playing with the levers. What he was thinking was probably borderline insane.

He pulled the one closest to the wheel and the forks lifted. He pushed it forward and it lowered. Easy peasy.

Wanda must have figured out what he was going to do and she tucked herself into a ball, as best she could. She was a big woman. Her smartest course of action would have been to try to get up again, but she seemed winded from her little run.

Jimmy slowed the machine even further and lined up the forks with the holes in the pallet. Then he pulled back on the lever.

Wanda was screaming and, despite the separation growing between them, Jimmy would have sworn she got louder the higher she was lifted.

"Jimmy!" Sara rounded the row of storage shelving and halted immediately.

Sean nearly ran into her.

Both of them started laughing.

Jimmy watched his friends put up their hands in surrender and spotted the flashing red-and-blue lights on the wall ahead of him. Someone had called the cops. This would be a fun one to explain, but at least his job with Tasty Beans had come to an end. And, of course, they'd caught a killer.

Chapter 50

Champagne and Brainstorming

The cops didn't really want to hear about their private investigator licenses and how a case from Albany brought them to Virginia and to Tasty Beans specifically. It had taken them a few hours to explain everything.

The contents of the bottle found in Wanda's purse tested positive for cyanide, and Adam's research of her online social profiles showed she had a love for photography and developed her own prints. Chemicals used in the process contain cyanide. A search of her residence confirmed that she had such a substance on her property.

More beans at the factory tested positive for the poison, including a few batches that Sara had worked on. She assured the police officer she had no intention of letting any ship. Based on their track record and reputation, he believed her. She was happy he was forgiving, as she wouldn't have been if any of it had slipped through.

Now on their jet, Sean requested they all be brought glasses of Cristal.

"Champagne? Are you flaking out on me, Sean?" Jimmy leaned back into one of the cabin's leather chairs.

"It's time to celebrate."

The stewardess returned carrying a silver tray holding three flutes of bubbly. She handed each of them a flute and then returned to the cockpit.

"What about Adam and Helen? They helped with this case too," Sara said.

"We'll just have to celebrate again once we get back. Any objections to that?"

"None here." Sara laughed and raised her glass in a toast, clinking it first to Sean's, then to Jimmy's.

"I've also been giving some thought to what we should name the firm."

"Really?" Impressive. He had helped take down a killer and he had a name suggestion for their business? She'd have to hear it before she got too excited. "What did you come up with?"

"McKinley Voigt Laverty Investigations."

Sara pursed her lips. "I'm not sure. What do you think of that, Jimmy?"

"That is worth celebrating."

Sara realized one person was missing off the name. "What about Helen? No Warner?"

"It's kind of getting a little long then, isn't it?"

"Sean."

"Well, I could put her name in big lettering on the wall behind her desk."

"That would be tacky."

"What about on the door under the company name?" This was from Jimmy.

"I don't know. I think she deserves a little more credit."

"We could give her a raise."

"She is great at compiling all the information on potential clients and sorting through everything."

"She is."

"Well?" She held eye contact with her husband.

"She's new to us."

She wouldn't relent.

"Fine. McKinley Voigt Laverty Warner Investigations."

She pressed the glass to her cheek. "You're right. It does sound a little long." She laughed.

The conversation lasted for the entire flight home. By the time they landed they still hadn't decided.

Chapter 51

It's All in a Name

Sophie Hogan entered the conference room of their PI agency, which, the next day, remained unnamed. They had called Sophie the day before to let her know that the person behind the poisoning had been caught. She had sobbed into the phone.

Today, she stood tall as she came toward them.

Sean and Sara were seated on one side of the table, with Jimmy across from them and Adam on one end. Sophie sat in the chair closest to the door.

"I can't thank you enough." Sophie pulled a checkbook out of her purse.

The door to the room opened and Helen took a seat beside Jimmy.

"We did this for you, for your mother, for all of Tasty Beans customers. But if it wasn't for you sticking to your gut feeling about your mother's death involving the coffee company, who knows how many others may have died," Sean said.

A tear trickled down Sophie's cheek, and she wiped it and nodded.

"That's the problem in the world today, people don't listen to their own voice. You did." He had discussed the matter with Sara beforehand, and there would be no mention of Susan Gallacher.

"What was the woman like who did this to her?"

"She was bitter." That was the brief summation.

What Wanda had said in her defense, if one wanted to term it like that, was that she deserved a big raise and was never given one. Paraphrasing her words, they were a million dollar company, growing larger every year, but when it was time for a wage increase they told her they wanted more for less. What they failed to realize or didn't care about, was that she saw what other people received and hers was nowhere near that. So, she said that she gave them exactly what they had asked for, more for less. More in their flavoring oils and eventually they'd get less in sales.

Sophie tore her signed check out of the book and handed it to Sara. "Worth every penny."

Sara passed the check to Helen, with a smile. "Helen will make sure the portions go to the charities noted on your application. Your mother would be proud of you."

"Thanks again." Sophie stood and let herself out.

Helen went to follow.

"Helen, after you see Sophie out, please come back," Sean said.

"Sure."

By the time she returned, Sean had pulled out a bottle of Cristal from under the table and popped the cork. Sara was walking back from a nearby cabinet with flute glasses.

"What's this?"

"It's time we give this firm a name," he extended a flute to Helen, "and we thought it best to discuss it as the team we are."

Helen's eyes misted. About six months ago, Mia, her six-year-old daughter was undergoing chemo and Helen had been on the verge of losing everything due to the high hospital bills. Jimmy didn't realize it, but Sean and Sara knew what he had done with the money they had given him.

"Do you have any ideas, Helen?" Sara asked.

She beheld each one of them. "I might. Since we need to peer into people's lives and spirit for motives, and we donate profits to charity, what about Pay It Forward Investigations?"

It hit Sean's ears and drilled straight to his heart. The hours spent discussing it on the plane were wasted.

Adam was bobbing his head. "As an abbreviation, it could also be P.I. Firm. Its simplicity is brilliant."

"Thank you." Helen was beaming.

"What do you think, Sara?"

"I love it."

"Let's do it then. To Pay It Forward Investigations."

Catch the next book in the McKinley Mysteries series!

Sign up at the weblink listed below
to be notified when it's available for pre-order:

CarolynArnold.net/MMupdates

By joining this newsletter, you will also receive exclusive first looks at the following:

Updates pertaining to upcoming releases in the series, such as cover reveals, book descriptions, and firm release dates

Sneak peeks of teasers and special content

Insights that give you an inside look at Carolyn's research and creative process

Read on for a preview of Carolyn Arnold's
next novella featuring Sean and Sara McKinley

SKIING IS MURDER

Chapter 1

It's All Downhill from Here

The snow-covered mountainside was glistening in the setting sun outside the window. It was so peaceful that it was hard to believe that a violent storm had passed through three days before and dumped five feet of snow. Luckily for Sean and Sara, all the runs had opened back up today.

They had gotten to Vail the previous evening. It was Monday now, and they were inside the chalet settled onto a couch and warming up next to the fireplace. Sara had her legs curled up beneath her, and Sean had his extended and crossed at the ankles.

He was sitting there thinking about how lovely the day had been. No murder. No mention of murder. Just him and Sara relaxing. Although they had retired their Albany detective badges when he'd inherited billions from Old Man Quinn, an elderly business tycoon, homicides were never far away. One murder after another kept dropping into their laps, starting on their honeymoon. They hadn't been looking for cases to solve, but after a year of it happening, they'd decided to make it official: they'd become licensed PIs and opened a firm.

Pay It Forward Investigations was opened about eight months earlier, and despite some zany cases they'd taken on so far, neither Sean nor Sara regretted the choice to become investigators. But sometimes they needed a little break from things. That was what had brought them to Vail, Colorado. Sean had sold Sara on the trip by saying it could be a pre-anniversary celebration—not to detract from the real date, which would mark two years of marriage the next month.

"You know that wasn't fair, right?" Sara lifted her glass of spiked hot chocolate and took a sip.

"Yes it was."

"It was not." She had a hardened look to her features, a concentration that usually showed when they were close to solving a murder. She flung her legs out from under her and angled her body to toward him. "You can't say 'race ya' while you're already taking off down the hill." Her words were full of heat, but her eyes were full of mischief.

"For the record, I never said 'race ya.'"

"Ah, Sean." She turned to face the fire and sat back, her eyes drifting to the flames dancing on the hearth.

"What I said was, and I quote, 'Whoever gets to the bottom last buys the drinks.'"

She leveled him with a glare, but the seriousness dissipated partway through the attempt. She was playing him, and her jig was up.

"I think I'll take a cognac after dinner tonight," he said. They were still a couple hours from that.

"Oh, what a lovely idea." She lowered her mug to a side table, and it wasn't long before a waitress came along and took it away. Sara declined the offer of a refill.

They had a full day of skiing, but Sean would be more than ready to hit the slopes again tomorrow morning. He appreciated the hum that was now vibrating through his muscles from the exercise. It invigorated him and even made sitting more enjoyable than it would have been if he'd done nothing physical during the day. He sank back against the sofa, letting his head rest on the cushion. He was so comfort—

"He's dead. I can't believe it, but he's—"

"It must have been an accident."

A nightmare? It has to be…

He must have dozed off. But sadly, when he lifted his head, he knew what he had heard was real. A group of five people had shuffled into the chalet, loaded down with ski equipment—three women and two men—and it was two of the women who had spoken.

"They say they found his body up on an advanced run," one of the men pitched in.

"I think I heard someone say it was Adrian Blackwell," the second man said.

"Adrian? He's an Olympic medalist." This from the third woman.

Sean's gaze went from one person to the next as the discussion volleyed among them. He tried to stay calm. Just because someone was found dead in the area didn't mean that he and Sara needed to get involved.

He reached for Sara's hand, but he couldn't find it. He pulled his gaze from the group to look at her. But she wasn't sitting there anymore. She was making her way over to the group.

No, no, no! He had to stop her before she reached them. They were supposed to be on vacation, not getting involved with any investigations. If a body had been found, let the local authorities handle it.

He shot to his feet and bolted after her. He caught Sara's arm on a backswing and then moved down to clasp her hand. "Sara."

She looked from his eyes to his hand. "Did you just hear what they said?"

I wish I hadn't.

He nodded. "But this has nothing to do with us." He scanned her face. "We're here to relax."

She smiled ever so slightly, the corners of her mouth barely curving. "I'm just curious." She cupped his cheek, the caress loving, soothing. Pacifying. And then she was off.

He was left standing there in the sea of people that had since gathered around the group spreading the latest gossip, and Sean felt his relaxing vacation slipping away.

Chapter 2

Harmless Curiosity?

She saw the look in Sean's eyes, the one that pleaded for her to leave the matter of the dead man alone. But she wasn't getting involved with the investigation; she was simply curious as to what had happened. From the sound of it, the deceased was Adrian Blackwell. He'd won two Olympic gold medals in skiing—one in 2010 and another in 2014. Adrian's death would warrant a full-blown police investigation, even if it appeared that an accident had killed him.

She always tuned in to watch both the winter and summer Olympics. There was something about the world coming together, united in the name of athletics. Political agendas seemed to fade. Nations became equals. Maybe that was why she always felt despondent when it came time for the closing ceremony. Maybe she was the only one who viewed the Games this way, but if she were looking at the world through rose-colored glasses, she'd keep them.

The friends were huddled together in a corner of the lobby, now surrounded by strangers hoping to get in on the news. After all, the average person rarely came across a death, let alone a potential murder, and the word *dead* seemed to spark attention and curiosity from most people.

Sara glanced over her shoulder at Sean. He followed her now, but it saddened her to see his solemn face. She stopped in her tracks and turned to face him.

"Do you want me to leave this alone?" she asked.

"You know I do."

Normally she would do anything he asked of her, but there was a burning curiosity within her that just needed to know what had happened. At this point, she had no inclination to get involved with the investigation.

She placed a hand on Sean's forearm, and he responded by tucking a strand of hair behind her ear.

"I just want to know what happened. That's all." She hated that there was a part of her—even if it was very minute—that doubted her resolve to leave it at *that's all.* Based on the tilt of Sean's head, he was questioning her intentions, as well.

"Are you sure? Because there's something in your eyes that tells me otherwise."

She was torn between getting more information and walking away. But Sean was the most important person in her life, and his happiness was her happiness. "We're here on vacation, Sean, and I know you've been looking forward to this trip since you first brought it up six weeks ago."

"I know you, Sara. I know us. For some reason, death is all around us."

"It's a good thing it's only *around* us," Sara said with a small chuckle.

He consented with a smile. "True enough. It could be worse."

She nodded. "If I promise just to find out what happened and leave it alone, can I talk to them?"

A few seconds of silence followed. She sensed he was almost offended—or ashamed—that she was looking to him for permission.

"I can't stop you, but please, let's stick to our plan of a

relaxing vacation," he beseeched.

"You got it." She slipped her hand into his, and the two of them joined the growing cluster of people.

As they approached, a blonde of about twenty-five was talking animatedly about where Adrian was found. She was one of the women from the original group. Her statement seemed to be in response to something a brunette in her late thirties had said as the latter bobbed her head.

The blonde caught Sara's eye. A man had an arm around her waist. His hair was blond like the girl's, but spiky. His bangs stood up as though he had done a face-plant in the snow, and his flushed cheeks supported that theory. "He probably OD'd," he said.

"Why would you go there?" The blonde turned to him. "He was a respected athlete."

"There's a lot of pressure on athletes." He added a shoulder shrug. "Maybe it got to be too much for him."

"I overheard the police say that it looks like an accident." This came from a young redhead. She wore her hair in two braids, and freckles dusted the bridge of her nose.

"Not buying it." A second man, a brunette who was also with the original group, adjusted his skis and poles under his arms.

"What do you mean you're not buying it?" The blonde leaned forward to look directly at him. "If that's what the police are—"

"The police aren't always right." The words came from Sara's lips without a thought, strictly on impulse. She cringed and didn't want to look at Sean. She could only imagine the scowl on his face.

Chapter 3

In the Hot Seat

Hey, do I know you?" The brown-haired man pointed a finger at Sara, then moved it toward Sean. "Wait a minute—" he snapped his fingers "—you're that couple. I saw you on TV."

Sara sensed the eyes of the thirtysomething brunette on her and met her blank gaze. Before looking away, Sara noticed the snowflake-shaped diamond earrings the woman wore. Stunning.

"They *are* the McKinleys!" The man was now adamant.

Sean tugged gently on Sara's hand, hard enough to make her take notice. But it was too late to retreat now. They'd been recognized and at least this young man knew they solved murders. It was surreal, as she often failed to appreciate that she and Sean were sort of celebrities. To her, she was just Sara McKinley, another human being on the planet. But ever since they had inherited billions, life had forever changed. They had loved each other before the money came into play but given the fact that they were partners, they didn't allow themselves to get romantically involved. But the windfall had allowed them to retire their police badges and get married. All these aspects seemed to fascinate people. Their continuing to solve murders when they didn't need to also may have led to them being interviewed on several major television networks.